Accidentally Forever

KATHRYN KALEIGH

THE ASHTONS
(Reading Order)

My Forever Guy

Our Forever Love

Forever Vows

Finding Forever

Accidentally Forever

ALSO BY KATHRYN KALEIGH

Contemporary Romance

Belonging in Alpine Falls

Stranded in Alpine Falls

Believe in the Magic of Christmas

The Princess and the Playboy

A Christmas Kiss on the Twenty-Fifth

Red Lipstick Kisses and Small Town Wishes

Stolen Chances and Big City Chances

Chance Connections and Upside Down Plans

Accidentally Forever

Finding Forever

Forever Vows

Our Forever Love

My Forever Guy

Out of the Blue

Kissing for Keeps

All Our Tomorrows

Pretend Boyfriend

The Forever Equation

A Chance Encounter

Chasing Fireflies

When Cupid's Arrow Strikes

It was Always You

On the Way Home to Christmas

A Merry Little Christmas

On the Way to Forever

Perfectly Mismatched

The Moon and the Stars at Christmas

Still Mine

Borrowed Until Monday

The Lady in the Red Dress

On the Edge of Chance

Sealed with a Kiss

Kiss me at Midnight

The Heart Knows

Billionaire's Unexpected Landing

Billionaire's Accidental Girlfriend

Billionaire Fallen Angel

Billionaire's Secret Crush

Billionaire's Barefoot Bride

The Heart of Christmas

The Magic of Christmas

In a One Horse Open Sleigh

A Secret Royal Christmas

An Old-Fashioned Christmas

Second Chance Kisses

Second Chance Secrets

First Time Charm

Three Broken Rules

Second Chance Destiny

Unexpected Vows

Begin Again

Love Again

Falling Again

Just Stay

Just Chance

Just Believe

Just Us

Just Once

Just Happened

Just Maybe

Just Pretend

Just Because

ACCIDENTALLY FOREVER
PREVIEW — RED LIPSTICK KISSES AND SMALL TOWN WISHES

Copyright © 2024 by Kathryn Kaleigh
Written by Kathryn Kaleigh.
Published by Kathryn Kaleigh Books 2024
Cover by Skyhouse24Media
www.kathrynkaleigh.com

This book is licensed for your personal enjoyment only. All rights reserved. This is a work of fiction. All characters and events portrayed in this book are fictional and any resemblance to real people or incidents is purely coincidental. This book, or parts thereof, may not be reproduced in any form without permission.

Accidentally Forever

Chapter One
GRACE MILLER

JUST ONE MORE PATIENT and I could call it a day.

I sat at my desk with my back to the window. On purpose. Too many distractions to try to work facing the window. I usually even lowered the shades when patients were in my office.

This fifth floor office had a clear view of the 610 West Loop looking out toward River Oaks. I couldn't see downtown Houston from here, but if I went up on the roof I could. From here downtown was so far away, it looked like a tiny cluster of buildings. Something a child might have built out of blocks.

No one went on the roof this time of year. Full on August in Houston was not the time for taking a break on the roof even if it had nice seating to enjoy the nice view. The building managers were talking about making the rooftop a green space with orange trees, but so far no one had moved in that direction.

Slipping my heels off, I rested my bare feet on the tops of my shoes. I wore what I considered appropriately conservative work attire. A dark gray pencil skirt with a matching blazer that hit at my waist. A white collared shirt. And of course, my heels.

I dragged the comb out of my hair and let my long hair swirl around my shoulders as I stretched my arms and got the blood flowing.

I had one hour to sit at my desk and catch up on notes for the day. I opened up my laptop and logged into the charting program my business partner insisted we use.

Me? I was okay with notes typed into a Word document and printed out supplemented by my handwritten notes neatly filed in folders and kept in a locked filing cabinet. A system that had served me well for the two years I'd had my own practice.

But going in with Jonathan had been a smart business move. He had more experience which meant he had more patients and not just that. He was on staff with the mental hospital and got frequent referrals. More than he could handle.

That's where I came in. I'd been with Jonathan for three months now and I was steadily building my patient load. At the rate I was going, Jonathan was going to have to bring in another psychologist before long.

He would have to lease another office if he did that and probably hire a receptionist. I had his old office and he had taken an empty larger one down the hall. There wasn't really space for a receptionist, but he would figure it out.

I was already working late at least three nights a week, one of them being tonight. I had to decide if I wanted to add Saturdays or another late night.

The office space was in a recently renovated building with

freshly painted walls and hardwood floors. Very clean. Very modern.

I tried to make sure my space wasn't intimidating. I kept a cinnamon and vanilla candle lit and fresh flowers, currently white daisies, on the corner of my desk. I personally preferred the scent of daffodils, but the florist had been out when I'd stopped by this morning. Daisies were fine though.

This side of the office was what I considered the working side. Desk and a small bookcase with books I used often including the DSM.

The other side of the office was the therapeutic side. Two comfortable chairs and a love seat. One of the chairs was mine. I let the patients choose whether they wanted to sit on the sofa or the other chair.

No coffee table between us. Just a big bookcase with books that were more likely to appeal to patients. Self-help books, mostly. A strong believer in bibliotherapy, I kept it well stocked with my favorite books that I tended to give away.

All part of the cost of doing business.

I was fairly fast at charting, so I was well into my last patient's notes when my phone alarm went off, reminding me to get ready for my seven o'clock patient.

All I knew about him was that he was a twenty-seven-year-old male. I usually had a diagnosis when they were referrals from the hospital, but this man had self-referred through our website.

I saved everything on the computer, logged out, and got ready for my patient. A cold bottle of water on the end table for the client. A new client intake form for me. It was just a habit to have it with me. I never looked at the intake sheets anymore. I had all the questions memorized and I was good at remembering what we talked about.

When the elevator opened, I glanced at the clock on the wall. My patient was five minutes early. I took this as a good sign.

Since people tended to get turned around coming off the elevator, I went to the door.

This man, however, was walking right toward my office.

Maybe walking wasn't quite the right word. Sauntering was a more accurate word.

Tall and lean, he was handsome with a sexy five-o'clock shadow that many men would envy.

As he sauntered toward me, pulling off aviator sunglasses as he walked, he struck a feminine chord deep down in my reptilian brain. I recognized the way my heart rate sped up and butterflies took flight in my stomach.

He's a patient.

I tamped down those primitive feelings of attraction and gave him my most professional smile.

In the process of tamping down my attraction, I felt myself leaning toward the other end of the spectrum. Extremely professional.

"Come in," I said. "Have a seat."

Chapter Two
BENJAMIN ASHTON

I VALETED my rental car at my buddy Jonathan's office building and headed straight for the fifth floor.

I could have taken an Uber from the airport, but sometimes I just liked the challenge of navigating city traffic on a busy freeway.

Since I had been here when Jonathan moved into this office building, I was more than familiar with the layout.

The spacious lobby with tall ceilings and bright chandeliers would be intimidating to a lot of people, but Jonathan—Dr. Jonathan Baker—didn't worry about such things. He was going for the high-end clients and did so unabashedly. Ambition was his middle name and from what I could tell, he was doing quite well in that direction.

The building had tall imposing live green plants placed strategically around as well as oversized furniture where people could wait for their appointments or just sit and use the WIFI.

The building held all sorts of professional offices. It had a psychiatrist, a chiropractor, a whole floor for attorneys, and a floor for some kind of stock trading.

The rent in this place alone required a certain level of clients. Apparently Jonathan knew what he was doing. The last time I talked to him—about six months ago, maybe longer—he'd been talking about expanding his business. Hiring on some help.

Not a bad idea, but I recommended he put an attorney on retainer.

Not only did I come from a family of entrepreneurs located in Pittsburgh, but I worked for Noah Worthington of Skye Travels. Skye Travels was the premier private airline company in the country.

Noah had taken one small airplane and built a billion dollar company on his own. He was a legend in the field of aviation. New graduates lined up at his door to be interviewed. I was no exception.

I'd been lucky. He'd branched out to Pittsburgh, and was looking to hire a pilot for there.

Long story, but it was around that same time that I learned that Noah Worthington was actually my grandfather's brother.

So he was Uncle Noah. An odd turn of events that had turned out well. The two brothers had gotten reacquainted after having lost touch with each other for most of their adult lives.

It was hard to think of him as Uncle Noah. Instead, I mostly thought of him as the boss.

At any rate, I knew a little bit about starting and running a business.

The elevator that took me up to the fifth floor had that fresh clean scent that smelled like success.

I should have called him. He often worked late, doing paperwork, but it was possible he had a client at this late hour. It was okay. I didn't mind waiting.

I stepped off the elevator into a wide carpeted hallway and headed straight for his office. Realizing I still wore my sun glasses, I pulled them off and blinked as my eyes adjusted.

I nearly came to a stop and would have except that my feet had unstoppable momentum.

A young lady stood at Jonathan's door. Maybe he'd hired some help already.

"Come on in," she said. "Have a seat."

Not one to argue with a pretty girl, I did as she asked.

She was a petite thing, even in high heels, dressed in a professional skirt and blazer.

Professional down to the white collared shirt.

I followed her inside the office. I recognized the view and although the office had the same general arrangement, things looked different.

The couch was new. One of the chairs. White daisies on a vase on the desk. A candle throwing out a mixture of vanilla and cinnamon scent.

Definitely different from Jonathan's décor.

I decided to try out the couch.

She sat across from me, leaning forward, holding a clipboard on her lap.

"I'm pleased that you came in," she said.

"Me too."

"I'd like to start with some basic questions. Then we can see if we're a good match and set up a plan of treatment."

A good match, huh? That was one part I was feeling confident about. As far as a plan of treatment, that sounded a little out of my league.

I glanced over my shoulder.

"I was expecting Jonathan to be here."

"He and I work together," she said. He's just down the hall. Since he's booked ahead several weeks, I was hoping you would give me a chance to work with you."

I realized right then that I was at one of those crossroads that could be life-altering.

The sensation was a little like flying an airplane. I made decisions every day that I hoped led to the best outcome. I had learned to go with my instinct and not second-guess myself. It had served me well so far.

"Okay," I said, giving her a little smile.

"I should introduce myself. I'm Dr. Grace Miller."

I was headed down that slippery slope and although there was still time to jump off, I was intrigued enough to play along.

"Benjamin Ashton."

A brief flash of confusion flashed across her face, but was quickly gone. She didn't recognize my name.

"I don't know much about you," she said. "Your application answers didn't go much further than you being twenty-seven."

"I like my privacy," I said.

Since I was playing along, I decided to be as truthful as I could.

"I understand. So do I. I have just some basic questions to get out of the way. Questions that will help me get to know you better."

"Go ahead," I leaned back, getting comfortable, and stretched one arm out across the back of the couch.

I'd been on a lot of dates. Usually getting to know each other was a little more subtle. Maybe this was a better, more straightforward way to get acquainted.

"Let's start with your occupation."

"I'm a pilot," I said.

"I see. A commercial pilot?"

"I work for a private airline company based here in town."

"Skye Travels?" she asked.

"Is there any other?" I asked with a smile.

"Not that I'm aware of. Do you have any siblings?"

She hadn't so much as glanced at the clipboard in her lap.

"I have two older sisters, one older brother, and one younger brother."

"You have a really big family. What was that like for you? Growing up?"

"I had a good childhood. Our parents were strict, but fair."

"You were close to your siblings?"

"Mostly my younger brother, but we were all close."

"What about now?"

"Now?" I ran a hand along my chin. "Now they're all married."

"And you? Are you married?"

"I'm single."

She didn't even miss a beat. Talking to her reminded me in

some ways of having a conversation with Jonathan. He was persistent also. Persistent and straightforward.

"What's it like being the only single person in your family?"

"They're all happy."

She leaned forward, looking into my eyes. Her eyes were a lovely shade of green. The color of a meadow seen from ten thousand feet in the bright sunshine of spring.

Her red bow shaped lips parted slightly, curved into a little smile that she seemed to be fighting a losing battle with. I could tell she was trying, rather unsuccessfully, not to smile.

"But what about you? What's it like for you?"

I shrugged.

"I now have two more sisters and two more brothers."

"You're close to your in-laws."

"We're all close. We all spend a lot of time together."

I opened my mouth to tell her that we all lived in the same house, but closed it. It wasn't something I told people quite simply because it was one of those things that was hard for people to understand.

It was hard for people to understand that our house was large enough to comfortably hold six families. Most people didn't even call it a house. They called it a manor—which it was.

I also didn't tell people that we had a cook, a gardener, and a housekeeper and all of them lived on the grounds.

Those were things I kept to myself.

"Tell me about your parents."

"They worked a lot, still do, but they always had time for us."

"They were supportive of your decision to become a pilot?"

I looked blankly at her a moment, then cleared my throat.

That was the other thing I didn't tell people. Not only did my uncle own the airline, but both of my brothers and both of my brothers-in-law were pilots.

"Yes," I said. "They are very supportive."

I was finding this conversation difficult. It was hard talking to her without telling her everything.

And even though there were things I didn't go around telling people, I wanted to tell her everything.

Chapter Three

GRACE

With the city ambiance that even drawn shades couldn't block out, I studied my new client.

I wanted to go back to my computer. I was decent at remembering names. I'd had it in my head that his name was Bradford... something. Not Benjamin. Maybe I'd read it wrong. But no. I distinctly remembered making a folder in the computer program with the name Bradford... something.

I'd straighten that out later. Couldn't very well jump up in the middle of a session to go to my computer because I was confused on his name.

So far I didn't see anything that would guide me toward a diagnosis. Jonathan would probably say he was enmeshed with his family, but I believed that to be a good thing. Families these days were too scattered and family support was one of those fundamental things that, in my experience, everyone needed.

When patients had family support, unless those families were completely dysfunctional, they typically fared much better than those who didn't have family support.

I had enough history from him for now. It was time to get some more pertinent information.

"Have you ever been hospitalized for mental health reasons?"

"No," he said.

"Have you ever had any kind of counseling?"

"No."

"You didn't indicate on your contact information anything that you might want to work on. Is there anything in particular that you'd like to talk about?"

He didn't answer right away. I gave him time to think. It was one of those thirty second pauses that seemed to last forever.

"It's just nice to have someone who listens."

If there was anything diagnosable about him, it was going to take some time to get him to talk about it. Private people were usually like that.

"It's hard for you to trust people," I said.

"I don't know if I'd go that far."

"But you don't have anyone you're comfortable talking to."

"I have a good friend. I talk to him."

"Yeah? When is the last time you spoke to him?"

"Christmas, I think. Maybe New Year's."

"So it's been about six months?"

"I guess so."

I wasn't concerned with that. It was typical guy behavior. Guys could go years without talking and still consider themselves good friends. When they picked up the phone, they just picked up the conversation like they had spoken last week.

It wasn't usually like that for women. I didn't like to generalize, but I saw it all the time. In order for girlfriends to remain girlfriends, they had to keep up with each other on a regular basis. Weekly. Sometimes even daily.

I had one friend, but he was a guy—also a graduate student.

Graduate school, then working didn't allow a lot of time for hanging out with friends.

The only people I'd gone out with socially during graduate school was fellow graduate students and all we talked about was psychology.

So I was in no place to judge Benjamin for going six months without talking to his best friend.

"What kinds of things do you do for fun?"

"I fly airplanes."

He said it without hesitation.

"I mean outside of your job."

"Occasional family time. A movie here and there. Grilling outside on family days."

"So no hobbies?"

"Flying is my hobby and my career."

"It's who you are."

"Yes." He sounded surprised that I understood that.

I knew what it was like to eat, sleep, and breathe one's career. It was what it took.

Having a career like psychology or aviation took complete focus.

My watch vibrated, telling me that we only had ten minutes left in the session.

"We only have about ten minutes left," I said. "So I'd like to go over what we talked about."

"Okay. Sure." He leaned forward and looked into my eyes. His eyes were a lovely deep cerulean blue that a girl could fall into.

How was it that a guy like this was still single?

Maybe that was something he wanted to work on.

"You're a pilot for Skye Travels. Flying is your passion. The one thing that's a constant in your life.

"You're close to your family. Two brothers, one older, one younger, and two older sisters. They're all married and you like their spouses. Am I right so far?"

"Impressively so."

"You have good family support and a good friend that you can talk to about just about anything. You're here because you just want someone to talk to."

"Yes," he said.

"Does this time and day work for you?"

He looked away for a moment. Gave me another one of those thirty second forever silences.

"I have an erratic schedule. I never know where I'll be."

"I can see where having someone to talk to could be a problem. Why don't you use the scheduling feature on the website to schedule your next session yourself. I'll recognize your name and I'll know you aren't a new client. Does that sound good to you?"

"It sounds okay to me," he said.

"So. Our time is up for now. Is there anything you'd like to add before you go?"

Clients invariably saved their true reason for coming to therapy for the last five minutes of the session. I always braced myself when I asked that question. I knew of psychologists had stopped asking for that very reason.

"Nothing to add," he said. "I enjoyed talking to you."

"Likewise."

He stood up from the couch and I stood up with him, holding my clipboard with both hands at my waist.

"Until next week then," he said.

"Next week. Whenever works for you."

"I'll let you know when I'm back in town."

"Take care, Benjamin," I said, walked to the door, and opened it.

"Good night," he said.

After stepping out into the hallway, I went back to my computer. I wanted to double-check his name. It wasn't like me to get the name of a new client wrong.

I went straight to the computer and logged in.

Ah ha. I had been right.

My client's name was Bradford.

And Bradford had sent an email asking to reschedule.

Chapter Four
BENJAMIN

I checked my watch as I stepped out of Dr. Miller's office.

I'd been in her office for fifty minutes, but it didn't seem like it. It seemed like I'd been there for about fifteen minutes. Time had flown by.

I stood in the hallway and considered. Jonathan had obviously moved his office. And he had obviously added someone into his fold. Just as he had said he would.

The problem at the moment was that I didn't know where to find Jonathan.

I walked to the end of the hall, checking names on doors as I went.

And there at the end of the hallway, I found his name on the door.

Dr. Jonathan Baker.

Since his door was closed, I sent him a text.

> Hey. I'm outside your new office.

He wouldn't answer if he was with a patient.
But he answered right back.

> JONATHAN
> I'm at the bar downstairs.

This day was just getting stranger and stranger.

> Do you want company?

> JONATHAN
> Sure. Come down.

Going back the way I came, I passed by Dr. Grace Miller's closed office. I was still a little dazed by that whole experience.

I had just gone through an entire counseling session.

I stopped, my hand almost to the elevator button.

Well hell.

I had just taken up an hour of her time that had been reserved for someone else.

That hardly seemed right.

I had to pay her for her time. For me the hour had been a casual interesting interlude, but for her, it had been work.

I never carried cash anymore, but I did keep one check on me for emergencies. I still, in this modern day and age, occasionally encountered someone who did not take credit cards, but oddly enough, would take a check.

Tugging the folded check out of my wallet, I wrote it out to her, leaving the amount blank, and signed it.

I wrote a note on the back.

I know I wasn't your scheduled client. Please fill in your rate for new clients.

I hesitated. I was running out of room, but I had so much I wanted to say. I boiled it down to the gist of it all.

Thank you for listening.

Feeling much better, I slid the check underneath her door and went straight to the elevator.

Maybe I'd have just one beer with Jonathan. It was early and I didn't have another flight until in the morning.

I needed to figure out just how much I was going to tell him about my hour with Dr. Miller.

Nothing. That's what I was going to tell him.

He'd probably tell me it was unethical pretending to be a client when I wasn't.

It wouldn't matter, or maybe it would make matters even worse, that I had enjoyed talking to Grace.

I got off the elevator, went outside, and walked across the street to the little bar where he and I had spent quite a few hours in our younger days. These days it wasn't like Jonathan to be here. He was typically home with his wife if he wasn't working.

But then again, as I had admitted to Grace, it had been six months since I had spoken to him. I had no way of knowing what was going on in his life right now.

He and I needed to do a better job of keeping up with each other.

I stepped into the upscale bar called simply *Equinox* and looked around for Jonathan.

The bar, a favorite hangout for the after work crowd was loud and the servers were hopping.

Jonathan, seeing me walk in, held up a hand and I spotted him across the room.

I slid into the booth across from him.

"What are you doing here?" I asked. "Why aren't you with Victoria?"

"Victoria left me."

Chapter Five
GRACE

AFTER MAKING a new file for my newest client, Benjamin Ashton, I charted the session and sent Bradford, my actual scheduled client, a message to reschedule.

I saved everything and powered off my computer.

Meeting with Benjamin had been a most bizarre encounter. I checked the scheduling website for his name, but he wasn't on it.

It was like he just randomly appeared at my office door. Being a bit flustered by the flutter he caused in my stomach, I hadn't done my due diligence in checking his identity.

Seriously, though, what were the odds that someone would randomly show up at my office who wasn't a client? And not just show up, but sit down and go through my series of questions?

That had never happened to me before.

It was possible, though. Our address was on the Internet. Maybe he had gone online, looked around, and just failed to make an appointment.

That was it, I decided. He'd just come up here, maybe to check things out, and I'd ushered him into the office. It was odd that he had shown up just when I was expecting a new client. Very unusual timing. But within the realm of possibilities.

I gathered up my things and headed to the door. It was time for me to go home. Past time.

I was looking forward to curling up on my comfy sofa with a romantasy novel I was deep into. It had been a long day and I needed a little escapism.

As I neared the door, I noticed something on the floor.

It was a folded check. Signed by Benjamin.

A blank check.

Well. This was most unusual.

I hadn't even thought about how he was going to pay. It hadn't occurred to me. When people scheduled on the website, they had to submit their credit card information and prepay. That was one nice thing about the website. We didn't have to worry about payment. I hated asking people for money after a session, so having that part of the process removed was an added benefit.

I would have to figure out what to do about this blank check from Benjamin Ashton. I dropped it into my purse to worry about later.

Minutes later, in the garage on the first floor, I got into my car.

I turned the key.

Nothing.

I tried again.

I seriously hated it when my mother was right. She'd been telling me that I needed to get a new car. I saw nothing wrong with my soon to be ten-year-old car. It had served me well and never gave me any problems.

Tonight, it seemed was going to be the exception.

I should just get an Uber and go home.

But. The nearest Uber was thirty minutes out. Since garages at night gave me the creeps, I scheduled one to pick me up at the Equinox, the little bar around the corner, but still in the building. A popular after work spot, it was always crowded. A good place to wait.

I locked up my car and hurried out of the garage. It had been such a bizarre day, I didn't want my mother to be right again. She was always warning me about being out late at night. Add that to the movies where people got attacked at night in deserted garages.

I chalked it up to my mother having never left the small town where I grew up and she still lived. But still. Strange day.

By the time I reached the bar, my heart was racing.

I went inside, into the safety of the crowd. A quick glance told me there were no available seats at the bar.

And I didn't see any available tables.

Then I saw Jonathan sitting at one of the booths. He saw me at the same time and waved me over.

As I neared, I saw that he wasn't alone. It was unusual for Jonathan to be out late. He'd gotten married less than two years ago and to my knowledge, he always went straight home. Maybe I didn't know as much about him as I thought I did.

It took a couple of minutes to wind my way through the crowd to his booth. I would only be there a few minutes, but at least it was a safe place to wait.

"Hi Jonathan," I said, reaching his booth. "I don't want to interrupt—"

Then I saw who his companion was.

Benjamin Ashton.

"Oh."

"Hi," Benjamin said, scooting over to make room for me to sit beside him.

"You two know each other?" Jonathan asked.

"Yeah," Benjamin said, scratching his chin. "About that..."

"Sit," Jonathan told me. "You look worried."

I dropped onto the bench next to Benjamin, but I spoke to Jonathan.

"Car trouble," I said. "I called an Uber, but..." I glanced at my watch. "It should be here shortly."

"What's wrong with your car?" Jonathan asked.

"I don't know. Won't start." I glanced at Benjamin who sat quietly next to me. I would deal with him next. One thing at the time.

"I hate it when my mother is right," I said. "She's been telling me to get a new car."

I'd been making some significant strides on paying off my student loans. I didn't need a car note.

"I can take a look at it," Benjamin said. "I know a little about cars."

"I'll have it towed to the garage in the morning." I automatically dismissed his offer, but that was another cost. This car thing was probably altogether going to cost me a month's salary.

"No need to do all that. At least let me look at it."

"It's too late. And I've got the Uber coming."

"Let me look at it in the morning then," Benjamin said. "Before you have it towed."

"I'd drive you home, but..." Jonathan said, holding up his whiskey glass. "I'm going to have to call for a ride myself."

"Cancel your Uber," Benjamin said. "I'll drive both of you home."

I looked from Benjamin over to Jonathan. He'd most definitely been drinking.

The server stopped at our table.

"What can I get you?" she asked me.

"Oh. I..." Sometimes the universe just flipped upside down and made no sense. This was one of those times.

A strange day that kept getting stranger.

Sometimes the only way to navigate a strange day was to just go with it. When paddling upstream, sometimes the only thing to do was to turn the canoe around and go with the current.

"A glass of chardonnay, please."

Chapter Six
BENJAMIN

I HAD some explaining to do.

That part was irrefutable.

But we'd get around to that.

Right now, though, wasn't the time.

My counseling session with Grace was between me and her. I'd already decided not to tell Jonathan about it. If she told him, that would be up to her. But I wasn't going to tell him. It felt too much like kissing and telling.

Dr. Grace Miller was most definitely kissable.

The problem was I'd gotten myself into a quandary.

With my best friend being a psychologist and all, I knew more than the average person about ethics. Specifically, I knew that a psychologist could never date a patient. That was one thing Jonathan never wavered on.

I had inadvertently, mostly through curiosity and what felt like a chemical attraction, made myself her patient.

I would have to fix that.

But right now, I was going to pretend to drink my beer while my best friend finished his whiskey and Grace—I didn't know how to categorize her yet—had a glass of wine.

Then I was going to drive both of them home.

Grace canceled her Uber and I could see her trying to figure out what was going on with Jonathan without asking straight out.

I also noticed that he didn't come right out and tell her that his wife had left him. Apparently that information was just for me. I didn't know what to say, really. I knew that Jonathan was insanely crazy about his wife. Tiffany. Her name was Tiffany.

Since he'd met Tiffany, I hadn't seen much of my friend. That seemed normal, though, to me.

Not more than an hour later, I got them both in my rented Maserati, fortuitously a four-door sedan instead of the sports car I had initially tried to reserve.

Jonathan in the front and Grace in the back. Not my idea. Jonathan just sort of automatically got into the front seat.

I had both their addresses programmed in. Since I was planning on staying over at Jonathan's house, I would take Grace home first.

After hopping onto the freeway, I looked in the rearview mirror at Grace. She sat quietly, looking out the window. I would have preferred to have her sit up front with me.

Grace lived in a townhome in an old, quiet neighborhood. I pulled up in front of her door, got out, and opened her door.

"I'll come by and take a look at your car in the morning," I said as I opened the gate leading up to her door.

"You really don't have to do that," she said.

"You'd rather have your car dragged into the garage so they can overcharge you?"

"Of course not." She shoved her hair back and put the key in the lock.

"Okay, then," I said. "What time do you want me to pick you up in the morning?"

"Pick me up?"

"Your car is at the office."

"I can call an—"

"Yes. I realize you can call an Uber," I said. "But, again, you don't have to do that."

"You've already done so much," she said. "Jonathan is the best friend you were talking about?"

That was the thing about psychologists. They never forgot anything.

"You're very astute," I said.

"Yes. Well. I don't know what Jonathan has going on right now, but I think maybe he could use your support."

I glanced back toward the car where Jonathan waited. He might be drinking tonight, but I had no doubt he would ask me about Grace. How I knew her for starters.

"You're probably right. Can I give you my phone number in case you change your mind?"

"I won't change my mind."

"Yes, well. Can I borrow your hand?"

"Why do you want my hand?" She asked, but she held up her right hand.

I pulled a pen out of my pocket, turned her hand over, and wrote my number on her palm.

"In the unlikely event that you need anything, call me. Deal?"

"Okay," she said.

"Either way I'll come by tomorrow. Fix your car."

"You'll fix it?" She ask with obvious skepticism.

"Probably. I'll look at it first."

"Good night, Benjamin."

She turned around, opened her door, and stepped inside.

Smiling to myself, I waited until I heard the lock click into place, then went back through the little gate at the front of her townhouse and got back in the car.

Jonathan had his head back and his eyes closed.

Maybe I'd dodged questions about Grace. With any luck, he wouldn't remember to ask me tomorrow either.

I pulled out of her driveway and merged onto the freeway heading back to his house.

"Tell me again how you know Grace," he said.

"I didn't tell you," I said. His psychologist tricks weren't going to work on me.

"You'll tell me later then."

But his best friend tricks stood a much better chance.

Chapter Seven
GRACE

After setting my keys on the table in the foyer, I flipped on the light in the kitchen and filled a glass with water.

Since I was rarely home, my house stayed clean with relatively little trouble. Unlike my office, I didn't often keep fresh flowers here. I was at the office far more than I was here.

I had very little furniture. I had a little bistro table for two in my breakfast nook. In the living room, I had a sofa and an end table. No television. If I wanted to watch TV, I had my computer or my iPad. About six days out of seven I chose a book over television or movies.

Although it was sparsely furnished, I felt at home here.

I typically came home, did whatever chore I had to do for the evening, and relaxed a couple of hours.

It was tempting to come home and work as I had done in graduate school, but. Therapist heal thyself was a good saying that enforced more often than not. Two hours to relax did not seem like too much to give myself.

While I drank the water, I stared at the phone number on my hand.

My skin still tingled where Benjamin had written his phone number.

This was quite the quandary I had gotten myself into with Benjamin. I had taken him on as a client, despite my attraction to him.

Everything was starting to make sense now. My best guess was that Benjamin had come to see Jonathan and found me in Jonathan's old office. I had swept him into my office and started treating him like a client.

He hadn't protested. That was the part I couldn't quite wrap my head around.

All he had to do was to say *Hey. I'm just here to visit Jonathan. I thought this was his office? Have you seen him?*

It would have been such an easy thing for him to do and it could have changed the whole trajectory of the evening.

My car still wouldn't have started and I still would have ended up at the *Equinox*. I still could have met Benjamin and he still could have driven us home.

But he… we… went and made it complicated.

He was my client now. I went to the sofa, picked up my novel, but didn't open it.

It had been a really long time since I'd had such an instant attraction to someone. In fact, I couldn't remember ever having such a strong instant attraction to anyone. Anyone I'd ever dated I'd simply… liked.

I think perhaps I had mistaken *like* for something more.

I thought this instant attraction thing was something I just read about in books.

But now... Now I knew it was a real physical and emotional phenomenon.

Tomorrow I would see if there were any journal articles on instant attraction in the psychological literature. One of my classmates in graduate school had done her dissertation on different types of love. I'd lost touch with her and didn't know what her findings were. Still. What I had experienced today was different from that.

What I'd felt was a visceral reaction. This was something entirely outside my realm of experience.

Maybe it was best that Benjamin was a client.

This kind of attraction could be dangerous.

I forced myself to open my book and start reading. This was my reading time and I was going to read.

Benjamin was outside of my orbit of potential people to date now anyway. Even if he never came back for therapy, I had established a therapeutic relationship with him.

Maybe I needed to talk to someone about this.

Maybe not.

Chapter Eight

BENJAMIN

I hadn't visited Jonathan much since he'd married Tiffany. I hadn't wanted to intrude on their newly married bliss.

She might not be in his house now, but she'd left a mark on the house. Curtains. I'd never known Jonathan to have curtains on his windows.

The kitchen was outfitted with a tea kettle—that was new—and a white tablecloth on the breakfast table.

One thing I appreciated, though, was their shiny new latte machine.

Up early, I made myself a latte and went out back to sit on one of their chairs. Their backyard was an oasis. It had lots of tall plants I didn't know the names for, but my favorite thing was their cocktail pool. The little pool doubled as a hot tub and a waterfall. It had a collection of boulders on one side with water sliding over the rocks into the clear somewhat shallow pool.

The scent of daffodils filled the air and a bird frolicked in the bird bath. Some more of Tiffany's additions. I couldn't see her getting out here and actually planting anything, but I could see her having it done. Looked like she kept the whole yard well-manicured. Again. Not the kind of thing Jonathan would worry about.

It was a relaxing place to sit and have morning coffee. To think.

I would not want to be out here in the summer, though. In the heat of the Houston summer. Something like this would be great for Pittsburgh summers though. Maybe I could plant the idea in my sister's head. As an architect, she could easily design one of these cocktail pools that would look great in our background. She could make the boulders blend in with the maple and pine trees.

Tiffany been gone for three days according to what I'd gotten out of Jonathan last night.

One minute he claimed he didn't know why she'd left and the next minute he said it was because he worked too much and was never home.

I thought they had worked all that out. My siblings had all hammered out that whole working thing. Pilots were gone a lot. It was just the nature of the business.

And Jonathan worked a lot. That was just who he was. Tiffany knew that when she married him. I'd even warned her at the wedding. But they had both been blinded by love.

Maybe some of the sheen had worn off. Or maybe there was another reason. I was inclined to go with there being another reason.

I had Tiffany's phone number so Jonathan might as well just deal with me calling her. Maybe ask her to have lunch. I wasn't going to just sit back and watch my friend suffer. Not without trying to do something to help.

It could simply be a misunderstanding. Easily fixed.

I would call her today after I finished fixing Grace's car..

She could take care of it herself, of course. She seemed like she was used to taking care of things by herself.

But it was an excuse to see her again. Maybe even spend some time with her.

I'd always had a thing for brunettes. Brunettes, single ones, were hard to find lately. Seemed like all the girls I knew wanted to be blonde, whether natural or not.

And her green eyes mesmerized me with just one look.

With Grace, though, it was the whole package. The long flowing hair. The red bow-shaped lips. The smile that she tried to hide.

She was a serious sort. I could see that about her. I rather liked it. She and Jonathan would work well together. They were both serious sorts.

Besides, I liked a girl who could do silence.

The girls I'd gone out with lately seemed to have a need to chatter. Chatter was fine and I liked chatter as well as the next guy. But there had to be breaks. There had to be times to take a minute and just think.

That need for the silence to think probably came from spending all that time alone in the cockpit of an airplane.

A side effect of being a pilot was a man became well acquainted with himself and if he didn't like his own company, then he was going to have a miserable life. Either that or find a job flying commercial where there was always someone sitting next to you. That sounded like hell to me.

I didn't mind the occasional person sitting with me in the cockpit. In fact, I enjoyed the company when I got it. But not every time.

My sister-in-law, a psychology professor, called flying and needing that time alone a positive addiction. I liked that and it struck a chord of truth with me.

I found myself imagining taking Grace up in an airplane.

I would enjoy her company.

I couldn't remember ever having a visceral reaction to someone like I'd had with Grace.

Just one look at her and I had been enchanted. I couldn't take my eyes off her.

It wasn't like me. I was twenty-seven years old and I'd had the opportunity to marry several times over. But I managed to keep myself aloof. I'd been attracted to plenty of girls, but I'd never been taken with one that I couldn't stop thinking about.

Unfortunately that had gotten me into a quandary.

I had set myself up as her client. Now I couldn't so much as ask her out without breaking her ethics code.

How many times had Jonathan told me about that whole can't date clients thing?

I don't think he even ever thought about doing it.

He'd met Tiffany at a charity function of some sort. Art, I think. She had nothing to do with psychology in any way. Probably could be a reason why, if that was the problem, that she didn't understand his long working hours. I still figured there was some other, simple, reason.

I checked my phone. Again.

Grace wasn't going to call. She was going to get an Uber to work this morning. I didn't blame her. First of all, she didn't know me. And second of all, and maybe even more importantly, I was her client.

I was going to end up talking to Jonathan about that. Maybe he had some magic solution to turn back the clock so that our session didn't count.

I hadn't meant for it to be a session. It had just been one of those moments. It had been like that split-second decision a person had to make when they were driving toward a yellow traffic light. Once committed one way or the other, we had to just go with it. There was no second-guessing allowed.

So I had run that yellow light... or stopped... I wasn't sure which way I wanted to go with that metaphor just yet.

Either way, it was time for me to take a shower and get ready to make my own way back to the offices.

I heard Jonathan up in the kitchen. He was going to have a heck of a hangover. Since I would be giving him a ride in to work this morning, maybe I could get him to talk about Tiffany. Once that problem was cleared up, I could make my way around to talking to him about Grace.

Not yet. I wasn't ready to talk about her yet.

I wanted to fix her car first. Spend some more time with her.

Before the clock struck Midnight and she told me in no uncertain terms that I wasn't to see her outside of her office. I had a feeling that if she didn't tell me, then Jonathan would.

I was determined to enjoy every possible minute with her until then.

Chapter Nine
GRACE

I MADE it to the office early. The sun was still making its way over the horizon in that beautiful way it had of diffusing the sky into shades of gold.

I'd been up early.

My first thought when I woke was Benjamin. He'd also been my last thought before I'd fallen asleep last night.

Maybe I needed to get on one of those dating apps and find someone who wasn't in psychology and wasn't a client or even a potential client to go out with. Maybe that would get my mind off of Benjamin.

Unfortunately, I couldn't get myself to think of going on a date with someone else. In fact, it had me feeling nauseated.

Ridiculous. I was being ridiculous.

And even though the sun wasn't even up, I was watching the door for Benjamin.

He hadn't said what time he would come by to work on my car. Just that he would.

I didn't have a client until nine o'clock. I didn't have to be here at seven, but here I was. I was worse than any schoolgirl hoping the guy she was crushing on stopped by her locker.

Looking at my palm, I saw his phone number still written on my hand. Maybe I'd been careful not to scrub at it. I liked it there. It felt like a connection with him. At any rate, I'd transferred his number to my phone as a new contact.

I'd slipped his blank check into my pocket with a plan to give it back to him when I saw him. If I'd been thinking, I would have given it back last night.

Did not accepting payment make the session not count?

I leaned back in my chair and sighed. Of course it did not. It was considered pro bono work. Payment or not, a client was a client.

With his check in my pocket and his phone number written on my palm, I felt surrounded by him.

Another glance at the door.

I was going to have to do something. I certainly couldn't continue to work with him. Not only would it be unethical, but I couldn't see myself working effectively with him. I was assuming that he actually wanted counseling. There was a distinct possibility that he didn't.

If he'd been looking for Jonathan, then I really had no good explanation for why he spent fifty minutes in my office.

Unless he was attracted to me, too.

If he was, what was I supposed to do with that?

I needed to focus. I had an email from a remote client I needed to answer. This particular client had opted in to supplement his every other week sessions with an email on in-between weeks. He lived in Katy and getting here was difficult.

We'd had no training on this type of therapy in graduate school.

What could I say? It was the modern world. Even psychologists had to be flexible and adapt.

I reread the email from my client. Made some notes about things I wanted to say in my response.

Another glance at the door.

Blowing out a breath, I got up, strode to the door with every intention of closing it. If the door was closed, maybe I could concentrate on my work better.

And Benjamin met me at the door.

So much for that.

"Good morning," he said, blocking the door, and smiling at me with that charming grin of his.

"You're here early," I said, my heart beating faster. He had that freshly showered scent and his short hair was still damp on the ends. Also his face was freshly shaved.

"Said by the one who was here before me."

I shrugged.

"Couldn't sleep?"

"Asked by the one who is here early."

He grinned and my heart turned upside down. When he smiled, the smile went all the way to his eyes.

He looked at me like he wanted to sweep me up and kiss me senseless.

Okay, maybe I was projecting on that part.

I wouldn't mind if he swept me up and kissed me.

He's a patient.

I reached into my pocket and pulled out the check.

"I can't take this," I said, holding out the check.

"Who says?"

"Says me."

"Okay." He tilted his head to the side, but didn't take it.

I shifted from one foot to the other. One thing I'd learned in my training as a psychologist was that the best way to say something was to just say it out right.

"I have the feeling that coming for counseling wasn't your intent."

He grinned again and I noticed the hint of a little dimple at the corner of his mouth.

"That obvious, huh?"

So I'd been right.

I shoved the check closer.

"I'll take the check back," he said. "but you have to let me fix your car."

Dangerous. Benjamin, client or not, was dangerous to my heart.

"Okay," I said. Really. What else could I say?

"Want to come down and show me which car is yours?"

"Right," I said, suddenly remembering why he was there. "Of course."

I went over, grabbed my keys, walked to the elevator with him.

I was wearing heels and he was still a head taller than me.

Somehow I hadn't realized that until I was standing right next to him as we stood waiting for the elevator.

Neither one of us said anything as we rode down the elevator to the garage.

"This is it," I said, unnecessarily since my car was the only one on the floor. "It's a good car. I haven't had any trouble with it."

"You don't have to explain it to me," he said. "Pop the hood."

First he checked the oil. One of the few things I knew about cars was how to check the oil and I only knew that because my grandfather had taught me that when he taught me to drive his old Chevrolet pickup truck.

"Oil's good," he said, mostly to himself as he screwed the top back on.

"Ah," he said after poking around a little more. "I see the problem."

"Really? Do I need to get it towed?"

He straightened and looked at me with an odd expression. "No towing."

"Can you fix it?"

"I can. But I have to go get a part."

"I'll get you my credit card," I said.

He put a hand on my elbow to stop me.

"Have you forgotten our deal already?"

I smiled, biting my lip.

"No. I haven't forgotten."

"Good." He held out his hand.

Not knowing what he wanted, I put my hand in his. Wrapping his fingers with mine, he looked at me with one brow raised.

"Keys?"

"Oh." Feeling silly I pulled my hand from his and handed him my keys. He slid them into his pocket, then let the hood drop.

"I'll let you know when I have it fixed," he said.

"Okay."

"Come on," he said. "I'll walk you back up."

"You don't have to do that."

"I don't have to, but I can."

I gave up. Benjamin was determined to walk with me back to my office, a trip I'd made a hundred times, so I'd let him.

It wasn't like it was a hardship. Walking with a handsome man.

Definitely not a hardship.

Chapter Ten
BENJAMIN

I TOOK my time getting the hose I needed to fix Grace's car. It was going to be an easy fix. Probably take no more than thirty minutes.

Traffic was heavy this time of day. Now I understood why Grace and Jonathan went to work early. To avoid fighting the traffic.

Navigating flowing traffic on the Interstate was entertaining, but sitting bumper to bumper at traffic lights reminded me why I loved flying so much.

I was a man who loved speed. And right now there was no speed. Just traffic light to traffic light.

Turning on the radio, I made the most of it and began to plot how I was going to get Grace to go to lunch with me.

If she wasn't available for lunch, I'd go for dinner.

I had to make my move today, though, because tomorrow I was scheduled to fly my client back to Pittsburgh.

The morning sunlight reflected off one of the high rises with walls of glass making a beautiful sparkly image. My sister Charlotte could easily capture that on canvas. The best I could do was to snap a photograph on my phone.

It was going to be one of those really hot Houston days. I hadn't checked the weather, but it felt like there might be a storm brewing.

Maybe it would hold off until tomorrow and I could delay my flight out of here.

I rarely wished for a flight delay. I blamed it on Grace.

A flight delay could mean more time with Grace.

Unless the clock struck Midnight and she or Jonathan put a stop to my pursuit of her company outside of the office.

I pulled into the parking garage and parked next to Grace's car.

My estimate that it would take thirty minutes to replace the hose was just about right.

The motor turned easily and hummed.

I turned off the motor, locked up the car, and headed up to see if Jonathan was available to hang out until lunch.

He wasn't. His closed door signified that he was with a client. Grace's door was closed, too.

By my estimation, they would both be out at ten fifty.

I had forty-five minutes to wait.

Finding a chair at the end of the hallway close enough to see their offices, I opened up my book to read a novel. I usually read on my iPad, but the phone would work in a tight.

The minutes passed quickly and I saw one client leave Jonathan's office, then another leave Grace's office minutes behind him.

I'd always wondered how they paced the sessions to end just at the right time.

It had to be an art combined with years of training, but it was most definitely impressive.

When the hallway was clear, I went to Grace's open door.

She sat behind her desk at the far end of the office her back to the window.

My heart swelled at the sight of sunlight spilling around her. Her hair was pulled back now, making her look elegantly professional.

She was wearing a skirt and blazer similar to the one she had worn yesterday except this one was in a light gray. She looked very stunning.

Her brow was creased as her fingers moved over the keys on her keyboard. She didn't see me at first, giving me time to soak in her features.

I was undeniably smitten.

It occurred to me then that even though I had spent one hour as her client, there was one thing that had been bugging me all along.

Who was going to know?

Chapter Eleven
GRACE

My ten o'clock client had been difficult. A woman who had been struggling with bipolar disorder for years. Recently released from the mental hospital, she was struggling to keep from sliding back down into depression.

I had to help her with her medication. Even though it wasn't within my scope of practice to prescribe, I did a lot of medication management.

Sometimes I felt like an educator. Sometimes like a cheerleader. Sometimes like a friend. Sometimes like a parent.

Looking toward the door as I'd been doing constantly all day, I blinked against the sunlight streaming in the window behind me.

Benjamin stood at the door, leaning against the door casing, watching me.

He smiled.

"Am I interrupting?" he asked.

"No," I said, although technically he was since I was almost finished charting my last client.

Seeing him standing there, I was suddenly none of those things I typically felt like.

I felt like a schoolgirl when the hottest guy in school showed up at her locker to walk her to class.

I closed the lid on my computer. There would be no more concentrating. Not with him standing there.

Walking over to my desk, he laid down my keys.

"It's fixed?" I asked.

"Good as new."

"That was fast."

"It took all of thirty minutes."

"I guess you are handy with cars."

"I'm pretty good with engines," he said. "When is your next client?"

I glanced at the schedule on my computer.

"One o'clock."

"Perfect," he said. "Let me buy you lunch."

"You just fixed my car," I said.

"And it took all of thirty minutes. I still owe you."

"You don't owe me." I should tell him no.

I should most certainly tell him no.

He's a client.

"Say yes," he said with a charming little sideways grin and a hint of that dimple.

"Yes," I said, trying not to smile back. "I'll meet you downstairs in ten minutes."

"I can wait."

I shot him a look and a little shake of my head.

"But I'll meet you downstairs," he said.

He seemed to catch on rather quickly. As Jonathan's friend, surely he knew that I couldn't get romantically involved with a client.

I could lose my license for it.

It's just lunch, I reminded myself as I logged off my computer and pulled my purse out of my desk.

Just lunch.

Unless he told Jonathan about our session, I could walk along the edge for a little while longer at least.

He lived in Pittsburgh. We'd have lunch and he would go on his way.

That was how it worked. I had nothing to worry about.

I'd keep it strictly professional. Keep the door open for him to come back for future sessions like I was supposed to.

I wasn't doing anything wrong.

Not that I could have resisted him even if I had wanted to.

No, I decided. I would refer him to a colleague. Not Jonathan because they were already friends. Someone else.

I'd tell him at lunch that I couldn't be his psychologist.

I wouldn't tell him that it was because I was attracted to him. I'd tell him that the other truth. That he was Jonathan's friend and I was Jonathan's friend and that meant the two of us would cross paths at a social level.

That was more than enough for a referral. It wouldn't work in a small town where I was the only psychologist, but here in Houston, it would.

Feeling like I was doing something wrong, even though I

wasn't, I kept an eye on Jonathan's door as I waited for the elevator.

As the elevator made its way to the first floor, I breathed a sigh of relief.

Just lunch.

It was just lunch.

Chapter Twelve
BENJAMIN

I PACED the lobby as I waited for Grace.

Although a couple of people walked along the sidewalk outside, I was pretty much the only person in the lobby.

One of the housekeeping staff walked along, pulling a little wagon, watering the potted plants, trimming the dried leaves from the head high indoor trees.

I paced past the concierge desk, the bank of three elevators, through the lobby, then started back again.

The concierge, an older man, paid me no attention. Maybe he'd seen me with Jonathan. Whether he recognized me or not, he mostly talked on the phone and tapped on his computer keyboard.

I stopped. Studied one of the trees.

A fig tree maybe.

The elevator doors opened and Grace stepped out.

She saw me and smiled. I pivoted and met her. Then turned again and we walked through the lobby together.

"Are you good with plants?" I asked.

"Plants? Why do you ask that?"

"Just curious. All these plants remind me of home. My youngest sister is an architect and she's good with plants. She knows where to put the tall ones and where the smaller ones look good. I would have no idea about those things."

"I like flowers," I said. "Not planting them, but I like them in vases."

"I noticed you had flowers on your desk." I said, holding the door for her. My car was parked out front.

"I think they make a home or an office look more inviting." I closed the door after she got into the passenger seat.

"Do you ever keep flowers at home, too? Or just at the office?" I asked, pulling away from the curb.

"Usually just the office. How did you know?"

"You're always at the office," I said with a shrug.

"That's true." She adjusted her seat belt. "Where are you taking me?"

"Where do you want to go?"

"Looks like we're headed toward Uptown."

"I know a little Mexican restaurant that has great tacos."

"Tacos are good."

I grinned and turned toward the taco place I knew. Jonathan and I had gone there several times over the years.

"When do you go back to Pittsburgh?" she asked.

I glanced toward the clear blue sky.

"Scheduled for the morning."

"I see." She nodded, keeping her expression blank.

"Do you work late tonight?" I asked.

"I'm not scheduled to."

"Want to go to dinner? Maybe catch a movie?"

"It's a school night," she said.

"And tomorrow I have to leave." I pulled into the Mexican restaurant parking lot. Found a place to park up front.

"What about Jonathan?"

"Jonathan is a big boy," I said. "He can take care of himself."

I turned off the motor and went around to open her door.

"Did you find out what was going on with him?"

"A little," I said. "But it's not my story to tell."

"Are you sure you're not a psychologist?"

The Mexican restaurant smelled like tacos and sizzling fajitas. Cilantro and cumin.

"My best friend is. And my sister-in-law. I consider myself well versed."

"Makes sense."

We followed the hostess to a table in the back. The restaurant was nothing fancy. No table cloths. Mostly just booths with lacquered tops. Brightly painted pictures on the walls.

Servers running here and there.

A margarita machine running behind the bar.

Next time I took her out, I was going to take her somewhere nice. Somewhere with live flowers on the table. White table clothes. Maybe live piano music. I'd have to ask Jonathan for a good place to take her.

Shortly after we sat, someone dropped off a basket of chips and two bowls of salsa.

"Have you been here before?" I asked.

"I don't think so."

"I'm a little surprised. Jonathan and I used to come here all the time."

"He and I don't really do lunch."

"How long have you known him?"

"He was a year ahead of me in graduate school. He was really helpful in getting our group placed at our internships."

"Sounds like him."

The server stopped at our table.

"Can I get you a margarita?" he asked.

"Just water for me," she said.

"Same for me."

"So now that you know all about me," I said. "Tell me something about you."

"There's not that much to tell."

"I guess I'll have to make it up then."

She settled back on her side of the booth.

"This should be fun."

"Okay. Let's start with what I know."

"I'm listening."

"Your mother thinks you should replace the car that got you through graduate school."

"She doesn't have to pay the note."

"And you are a very logical person. Where is your father in all this?"

"He does whatever my mother wants him to do."

"Which is?"

"He cooks. Does all the housework."

"So your mother works?"

"She has an ecommerce business. He works, too, but he works from home a lot."

"Who doesn't these days?"

"True. He does his job, takes care of the house, and helps her with her business."

"Your father sounds like an impressive man."

"He is. They're both impressive."

"Brothers? Sisters?"

"I have an older brother. He's a psychiatrist. Lives in Boston."

"Just the two of you?"

She nodded. Broke off a chip and dipped it cautiously into her bowl of salsa.

"So both of your parents' children went into mental health."

"A little strange?"

"I don't think so."

Our server interrupted our line of conversation by taking our order. We both ordered shrimp tacos.

So far this was going much better than I had expected.

I wasn't supposed to date her, but it felt like a date.

Jonathan would say that if it quacks like a duck, it was a duck.

I'd always had an affinity for ducks.

Chapter Thirteen
GRACE

The tacos here were some of the best I'd had.

I was a little hurt that Jonathan hadn't at least mentioned it to me. He was private though.

I hadn't even been invited to his wedding, also small and private. Of course, that was before I went into business with him so I didn't take offense.

Being with Benjamin felt easy. He was good at carrying a conversation about nothing while at the same time he managed to get me to talk about myself.

I rarely revealed personal information about myself during a session. Only when it seemed relevant and/or furthered the therapeutic relationship.

But this wasn't a session. It also wasn't a date even though it felt a little—maybe more than a little—like one.

I decided it was somewhere between a casual lunch with a

friend and a session. I was determined not to let it slip into that dating area, no matter how much it felt like it could.

"What does your other sister-in-law do?" I asked. "The one not a psychologist?"

"She works with my brother. Not as a pilot, but she flies with him a lot."

"He's a pilot, too."

"He is."

"So you have two pilots in the family."

"Five actually, counting myself."

"Five."

"Both my brothers are pilots and both of my brothers-in-law."

"Wow. Your family sounds like mine, only bigger." I didn't know of very many large families anymore and I'd never heard of a family with five pilots.

"Is your father a pilot, too?"

"No." He pulled out his credit card and handed it to the server.

"How do your parents feel about having all you as pilots?"

"I don't think it bothers them. It runs in the family blood."

"There are others?"

"My grandfather was a pilot for a while. He's into real estate now. My uncle is also a pilot."

"I'm officially impressed. Did you ever think about doing anything else?"

"Never. It wasn't expected of any of us. We just all gravitated toward it."

"Interesting."

"Thinking about doing a case study?"

I laughed. "Case studies aren't really my thing."

"Too bad. Sometimes I think my family needs to be analyzed."

"Don't they all?"

Back in the car, on the way back to the office, he circled back around to our earlier conversation. Maybe he had psychology running through his blood as well as aviation.

"What time can I pick you up for dinner tonight?"

"Like a date?"

"I promise not to call it that."

I hid a smile behind my hand.

Benjamin was slick. I had to give him that.

But he was also charming. Dangerously so.

Even if he didn't call it date, I knew it would be.

What we called it wasn't necessarily the problem.

The problem was that no matter what we called it, I wanted to spend time with him.

I wasn't supposed to do that.

He was a client.

It also just plain wasn't a good idea.

Tomorrow he would go back to Pittsburgh.

The more time I spent with him, the harder that was going to be on me when he left.

Chapter Fourteen
BENJAMIN

Since I had an afternoon to kill, I went for a walk in the Galleria.

I would have preferred to go for a walk in Memorial Park, but the Houston heat was prohibitive.

So I sat on a bench at the ice skating rink and watched people at all levels of skill out on the ice.

There were some people who could barely stand up on their skates and there were others who swirled about on the ice as well as professionals.

I gave some thought to renting some skates and going for a spin, but decided against it.

It was too crowded out there.

I could hold my own on the ice. Eight years of hockey. High school, then college. Sometimes I wondered if I could have gone pro.

But it hadn't been part of my plan.

I'd wanted to be a pilot for as long as I could remember. Making my career on the ice wasn't part of that plan.

It would have sent my life in a whole different direction.

I was content doing what I did.

And I never would have met Grace if I had adopted the pro hockey lifestyle.

I had the disconcerting feeling that my whole life had been slowly leading me toward meeting her.

She had agreed to dinner with me tonight.

That was an unexpected gift.

Her only caveat was that I could not call it a date.

I was okay with that.

We could call it whatever she wanted to. We didn't even have to give it a name.

At any rate, I was supposed to pick her at her house up at seven.

It was definitely a date.

But as far as I was concerned, that was just between her and me.

Jonathan could talk to me on the phone later if he wanted to. Like I told Grace, Jonathan was a big boy.

Tiffany hadn't answered her phone, so whatever was going on, she didn't want to talk to me.

I'd left a message. I really hoped she called me back, but I was beginning to think that it wasn't any of my business.

That could have something to do with me finding Grace and making her my business.

It would be impossible for me to solve Jonathan's problem

and take Grace out on our not-a-date date tonight. It was a choice I had to make. Jonathan or Grace.

It was already bad enough that I had to leave in the morning.

Unfortunately, I had responsibilities.

When my phone rang, I answered right away, thinking it was probably Tiffany.

But it wasn't Tiffany. It was Mary calling from Skye Travels.

"Benjamin?" Mary said. "Are you available to take a flight?"

"I have one in the morning."

A child wailed as his mother picked him up from the ice where he had fallen. I covered my right ear and pressed my phone closer to my left.

"No," she said. "Today. As soon as you can get to the airport."

"I'm scheduled for tomorrow," I said again, trying not to sound annoyed.

"Someone else can bring Mr. Fontenot back tomorrow. We need you to take an emergency flight out today."

"Today." I was having trouble engaging my brain. My usually quite flexible brain.

In this case, all I could think about was my date with Grace.

"Can you be at the airport in thirty?"

"I'm at the Galleria." A lifeline of hope that I was too far away.

"Just get there was soon as you can."

"Text me the information."

Mumbling something incoherent, I disconnected the line with a knot in the pit of my stomach.

I didn't have to tell her to text me. I knew the drill. She knew the drill.

What I couldn't see was a way out of it.

Chapter Fifteen
GRACE

I spent the afternoon keyed up. My last client, at four o'clock, fortunately was an easy one as far as patients went. She had been through a bad divorce, but she was getting her feet back under her. Had a job. Her mother was keeping her child while she worked.

She had a date this weekend that she had been looking forward to. She'd met the guy on one of those dating apps.

"Using the dating app has been a good experience for you?" I asked.

My client, a woman in her early thirties, was attractive and wouldn't have any trouble getting dates once she started getting out there.

"It's been okay," she said. "It helps me sort through a lot of people without having to actually meet them."

"It's efficient," I said

"Yes. And kind of fun." She said it with a little shrug as though it shouldn't be fun.

I imagined it was a dopamine hit, too.

"Well. I'm looking forward to hearing about how it goes."

"So many possibilities." She beamed.

And so many landmines. I would make sure to remind her that my door would always be open to her. I had a gut feeling that she was still vulnerable and would experience some heartbreak before she got into her next stable relationship.

As I charted my notes on the session, I wondered again if maybe I should check out one of the dating apps.

And again, I didn't have the stomach for it.

I was still too excited about having a date—but not technically a date—with Benjamin tonight.

I wasn't supposed to be dating him.

He was a client.

But that didn't seem to matter.

It was that strong visceral attraction and I'd never experienced anything quite like it.

I finished up my notes and powered off the computer.

I had two hours to get home, shower, figure out what to wear, and do my hair and makeup.

I was never going to make it.

Grabbing my purse from my desk drawer, I hurried toward the elevator. While I waited for the elevator to arrive, I checked my messages.

Nothing from Benjamin.

I could still see his number written on my hand. It was fainter than it had been this morning, but I could still see it.

It occurred to me then that although I had his phone number, he didn't have mine.

If I called him he would have my number.

But I didn't have a good excuse for calling him.

I needed an excuse before I called him.

The elevator door opened and I stepped inside.

The clock was ticking and traffic was not on my side.

As I drove, I did a mental assessment of my clothes and tried to figure out what to wear.

Why was it a girl never had anything to wear on a first date?

Not a date, I reminded myself.

Under any other circumstances that did not involve ethics, it would be a date.

I felt myself sliding down a slippery slope.

I have never—not even once—been the least bit tempted to date a client. It just wasn't something I did.

It had been drilled into my head from day one that it wasn't allowed.

Benjamin was different. Every psychologist in the history of psychologists who had ever been tempted to date a client, I was certain, said the same things.

It was human nature to think that we were unique.

I'd written down the name and number of the psychologist I was referring Benjamin to. So that was one thing taken care of. Making sure he had someone to talk to just in case he did.

But Benjamin really was different in that he was Jonathan's friend. He hadn't even sought me out for counseling.

Although he hadn't said as much, I had no doubt that he had just gone along with me when he'd walked into my office.

It was a simple case of mistaken identity.

That could be my defense to the ethics committee.

I had a thought that kept nagging at the back of my mind.

Although I had seen Benjamin for a session, if there was no record of it, then it never happened. That was the rule of charting. If it isn't in the chart, it didn't happen.

He wasn't scheduled. He hadn't paid me. I wouldn't see him again.

I could say that he and I had simply been having a conversation while he waited for Jonathan.

The only thing that could go awry would be if either Benjamin or even Jonathan—if he found out—decided to file a complaint.

I couldn't see either one of them doing that.

So the bottom line was quite simple.

Who would know?

Chapter Sixteen
BENJAMIN

While I was driving to the airport, however reluctantly, I worked on sorting out how I was going to get in touch with Grace to let her know that I had to cancel our date that wasn't a date.

She had my phone number, but I didn't have hers.

The simple solution was to call Jonathan. Get her number from him.

Geez. I did not want to explain this to him.

But it seemed like my only option.

I could tell him that I'd worked on her car, he knew that, and I wanted to make sure it had started.

Jonathan was no fool, but since he was focused on his own relationship with Tiffany right now, that might distract him enough to buy me some time.

As I zipped over in the fast lane behind a silver sports car, I asked Siri to dial Jonathan's number. It went straight to voicemail.

He would be in with a client. I'd never known him to turn off his phone for any other reason.

This left me in quite a dilemma. I had given Grace my phone number, but I didn't have her number.

I had no way to call her.

After I pulled into the rental return parking area, I checked my phone again. No messages. No missed calls.

I didn't have time to drive down there to tell her that I had to fly out tonight. That would have been a good idea before I drove all the way up here to the airport.

It was too late now. My passenger was already waiting for me.

Grace didn't know me well enough to know that this was the way of life with pilots.

She was going to think I'd stood her up.

And I had, but not on purpose.

It wasn't something I would do on purpose. Certainly not to Grace.

After I dropped off the rental car, I tried Jonathan again. He wasn't answering his phone.

All I could do was to call him again after I landed in Pittsburgh. It would be late.

I wouldn't blame Grace if she never spoke to me again.

Surely she would understand. She seemed like a very understanding person.

I'm not sure I would understand if the shoe were on the other foot.

Walking out onto the tarmac toward my plane, surrounded by the scent of jet fuel and the sounds of engines as they prepared for takeoff, I knew I had no other choice.

Grace didn't work in the kind of office that had a receptionist. Other than her cell phone, there was no other way to get in touch with her.

I was standing up the girl of my dreams.

All I could do was to hope for forgiveness.

It wasn't my fault.

As I sat in the cockpit of my little Cessna, I tried Jonathan's phone one more time.

It was a quandary.

I wasn't ready to tell him about Grace. If I left a desperate message asking him to call her. To tell her I couldn't make it, he would know.

It was out of my hands, so I went with my gut.

I would fix it. Tomorrow. I would fix it tomorrow.

Chapter Seventeen
GRACE

Seven o'clock came and went. I paced my little townhouse, keeping myself busy with straightening things up as I went.

I'd decided on a flowy skirt and a lightweight sweater perfect for a night out. I was a little surprised, pleasantly so, to find that I still had what I considered date clothes in my closet.

I put a load of laundry in the wash.

I made sure all the dishes, mostly glasses, were out of the sink and hidden away in the dishwasher.

Sitting on my sofa, I went through and deleted all the emails I didn't need.

With that done, I got up, went to the window and stared out the sky splashed with an array of reds and golds.

By seven thirty, I knew he wasn't coming. I already knew it, but that's when I went ahead and changed out of my sweater and put on a t-shirt.

As I made myself a cheese and tomato sandwich, I began to worry. What if something had happened to him? I would have no way of knowing.

I unlocked my phone, scrolled to his number, held my breath, and dialed.

It went straight to voicemail.

I would never understand people who turned off their phone. Even when I was with a client, I turned my phone on silent and left it on my desk. At least with it on, I could get my missed calls.

With the phone off, if someone called, I wouldn't know it.

The whole purpose of a cell phone, in my mind, was to not miss anyone who might need to get in touch.

I didn't leave a message. I disconnected the line and ate my sandwich at my little dining table.

It was for the best, I told myself.

The best thing that could have happened.

By not showing up, he saved me from myself.

And probably saved my career at the same time.

Because no matter how well a person thought they covered their tracks, they never really did. Someone always found out.

And since Benjamin and Jonathan were good friends, Jonathan would find out.

I could only see that going badly.

So I went to my reading sofa, untied the little boots I'd been wearing, and forced myself to read.

I made it through three pages before I gave up on trying to concentrate.

Frustrated with the whole situation, I googled dating apps, picked one that sounded good, and downloaded it.

I quickly entered my information. Put in some basics and waited for something to happen.

Within fifteen minutes, I had three matches.

I'd been right about the dopamine rush.

Glancing over their profiles, I immediately dismissed the matches.

None of them were private airplane pilots from Pittsburgh with a five o'clock shadow and eyes of blue.

And right now that was just about all I had bandwidth for.

I was something of a mess and I could admit that to myself.

Tomorrow I would suck it up and talk to Jonathan. Explain the situation.

That was the first thing we were supposed to do in a situation like this. Consult with a colleague. Someone more objective about it all.

Jonathan might not be objective, but he would be more objective than I was about it.

I should keep notes.

Opening up the iPad I kept for reading digital books I got from backing author's Kickstarters, I started a new notes page.

I needed to document everything that had happened so far with Benjamin so that if there were an inquiry I would have accurate information.

By the time I had everything written down, I felt better about it all.

I was human, after all. A red blooded American girl. What red blooded American girl wouldn't be attracted to Benjamin Ashton, pilot?

I saved the file and decided to give myself a break just as I wouldn't judge any one of my clients.

Not a day went by that I didn't sit in my office and instruct clients on this very thing about forgiving oneself.

It might be easy enough to forgive myself, but it was going to be a whole lot harder to stop thinking about Benjamin.

Chapter Eighteen
BENJAMIN

My flight to Pittsburgh was uneventful. An uneventful flight, of course, was the best kind of flight.

The skies were clear blue with white puffy clouds here and there. No rain on the radar at anywhere along my route.

My passenger stayed preoccupied with his own thoughts. I didn't ask what the emergency was and he didn't say. I would listen if he wanted to talk, but otherwise it wasn't my business.

I took my own car, a Maserati, I'd left parked at the airport to my family home.

Turning off the main road onto the private drive, I felt some of the tension begin to drain away. Home was a place where I could relax. Outside of being in the cockpit of an airplane, it was the best of places for me to relax and think.

Being here was different from flying in that here I was rarely left alone. Instead, I was surrounded by family. Being surrounded by family was a unique healing experience all in itself. I couldn't imagine having to go through life without my family even if they did get on my nerves sometimes.

I parked and went in the back door. Followed sounds of life to the living room where my younger brother Henry and his wife were playing UNO with my youngest sister, Bella, and her husband.

"The prodigal son returns, " Henry said as I walked by on my way upstairs.

"Funny," I said, pausing at the door to watch my sister shuffle and deal cards like a professional card shark.

"Thought you were coming home tomorrow."

"So did I," I said. "Emergency flight."

"You don't look happy about it," Bella said, setting the deck of cards in the middle of the coffee table and turning the top one up.

"Supposed to stay until tomorrow," I said. "Doesn't matter. Good night."

I continued on my way upstairs. I knew how this worked. They would keep it up until they found out just why I didn't look happy about coming home early.

I didn't feel like talking about it. Not tonight anyway.

Closing myself in my room, I sat down at my desk and checked my phone. No messages.

It was too late to call Jonathan and I didn't have any missed calls. Didn't mean that Grace hadn't tried to call me. My little Cessna didn't have WIFI, so if she called, I wouldn't know it unless she left a message.

What had started out as a perfect day had fallen apart by no fault of my own. No fault of anyone's really. It just had. Work. It was a work thing.

It was nothing that couldn't be fixed. Hopefully.

I logged into my flight schedule and checked my upcoming flights. Nothing to Houston.

No breaks either for the next two weeks.

I closed the computer. There was no way I was going to get back to Houston anytime soon. It wasn't exactly on my route. Not too many people wanted to fly from Pittsburgh to Houston. Most people on my normal route wanted to fly to Chicago or Indianapolis. Or Philadelphia.

I googled Grace's name but didn't find anything on her. Even googling Jonathan's name didn't lead me to her.

She was one of the few people I knew who managed to fly below the Internet radar.

I would figure something out.

I just needed time.

Chapter Nineteen

GRACE

THE NEXT MORNING I woke feeling slightly disconcerted. Usually when I woke in the mornings, I woke feeling positive. When anything seemed possible.

I always liked to think that I had as many hours ahead of me in my day as everyone else.

After making myself a cup of coffee, I sat down at my breakfast table and opened a notebook where I made notes every morning. I liked to write down my thoughts before they got cluttered by the day.

I had a system.

Something I needed to do. Anything that was bothering me. Something to look forward to.

Turning to a fresh sheet, I dated it and without thinking too much, I wrote down one thing I needed to do today.

Talk to Jonathan.

Sitting back, I sighed. It was not exactly something I looked forward to doing, but it needed to be done.

Order new book to read.

There. That was better. Something I needed to do and something to look forward to.

Then I wrote down the thing that was bothering me.

That was easy.

Benjamin Ashton.

In the light of day, things didn't look so bad. Jonathan would know if anything had happened to him. Benjamin was staying with Jonathan.

Another reason to talk to Jonathan.

Now that I had my marching orders, I got ready for work and headed to the office.

As was typical, I was the first one there.

It was usually a tight race between me and Jonathan.

Since his office was on the other end of the hall, I wouldn't see him come in.

After I got my office ready for the day, I walked to the elevators and turned left to where I could see his door.

He wasn't in. He only closed his door if he had a client and he didn't have anyone on his schedule until nine o'clock.

Sometimes he did rounds at the hospital first thing in the morning, but I didn't have access to that part of his schedule.

I ducked into the restroom before heading back to my office.

I didn't mind catching him later. The problem was the longer I put off talking to him, the easier it would be to do so.

After taking my time washing my hands with soap that

smelled like peppermint, I checked his door again. Still closed. Then headed back to my office.

Halfway across the room I stopped. The white daisies that still sat on my desk, were overshadowed by a large vase of red roses.

Forcing my feet to move again, I leaned in to breathe in their sweet scent, then counted them. There were twelve of them. Perfect dewy little red buds.

I pulled the card out and took it with me around the desk.

Dear Grace,

Please forgive me. I didn't have your number.

I had to fly someone to Pittsburgh at the last minute—an emergency flight.

Call me or send me a text.

Benjamin

I reread the note three times.

It had been right. There had been a logical explanation.

My phone chimed again.

Another match on the dating app.

I considered myself to be in touch with popular culture, but I hadn't realized just how many people used these dating apps.

I had half a dozen matches and I'd only signed up last night.

Ignoring the notifications, I pulled up Benjamin's number and began composing a message.

I typed. Deleted. And typed again.

Finally satisfied with my message I hit send.

> Hi. It's Grace. Thank you for the flowers.

Simple and straight to the point usually worked.

I got an almost immediate response back.

> **BENJAMIN**
> I hope you can forgive me.

> I understand.

> **BENJAMIN**
> I tried to call Jonathan to get your number, but he didn't answer his phone.

> Did you leave a message?

> **BENJAMIN**
> No. I didn't want to have to explain.

I blew out a breath. That was a relief. And to think that I had almost talked to Jonathan about Benjamin.

> He isn't in yet.

> **BENJAMIN**
> I'm a little bit worried about him.

> Should I be?

Another match came through on my phone's dating app. Good grief. Seriously?

I was going to have to delete the app.

> **BENJAMIN**
> He'll be okay.

I was curious about what was going on with Jonathan, but his personal life wasn't my business.

Walking down the hallway again, I saw that his door was still closed. It was eight thirty and he wasn't here yet for his nine o'clock appointment.

He was usually here by eight, but he could have gotten tied up at the hospital.

He would show up soon. Jonathan was nothing if not responsible.

Going back into my own office, I checked the scheduling app. I had a client that wanted to reschedule. Another one who wanted a last minute session.

I really hoped Jonathan got that receptionist soon. I liked having control over my own schedule, but keeping up with everything involving the new influx of clients was getting a little out of hand.

I took care of those things, then went back to check on Jonathan's door one more time.

Then I had to focus on my own clients.

His door was still closed.

He had ten minutes to get here.

His first client, in fact, was waiting for him.

I knocked on Jonathan's door. No answer.

Using my key I unlocked his door and stepped inside.

He wasn't in.

I pulled out my phone and dialed Jonathan's phone number.

It went straight to voicemail.

I had a client at nine and so did Jonathan.

I went out to where Jonathan's client, a middle aged man with gray hair, waited.

"Hi. I'm Dr. Grace Miller. I work with Dr. Baker."

"Hi," he said. "I'm Trent."

"It's nice to meet you Trent. Dr. Baker seems to be running a little late today."

"That's okay. I can wait."

"Good," I said. "That's very understanding of you. I have a nine o'clock appointment, too. Do you mind if I take down your contact information. If he isn't here in fifteen minutes or so, I can reschedule you. I don't want you to have to wait too long."

"Sure," he said, then gave me his phone number. "I hope he's okay."

"I'm sure he just got tied up at the hospital," I said.

But as I walked back to my own office, I worried. Jonathan was late and he should have called me by now to reschedule his client. In fact, he probably could have contacted Trent directly.

Any number of things could have happened.

I couldn't worry about it right now though. I had my own client who needed my undivided attention.

I put my phone on silent and left it on my desk.

Everything would work out just fine.

Chapter Twenty
BENJAMIN

Breathing in the early morning scent of jet fuel was a good way to start the day.

I had to make a quick flight over to Philadelphia to pick up a passenger, so I was at the airport early.

I'd had to pull some strings to get the flowers on Grace's desk before her day started. I couldn't let her go any longer without hearing from me. Not when I had so clearly stood her up.

The flowers had been a burst of inspiration that I'd gotten when my brother had told me he was having flowers sent to his wife for her birthday.

I'd had to pay double to get them delivered so quickly, but it had been worth it.

Now I had her phone number.

The air traffic controller's voice came through my headset giving me permission to takeoff.

Another benefit of taking an early flight. The runways weren't backed up with flights so things moved more quickly.

My wheels left the ground and I knew the moment I hit ground effect. Hitting ground effect was by far my favorite part of the flight.

It was that moment when the airplane left the ground and I was airborne. I left the world behind and it was just me flying like an eagle.

I stayed busy monitoring the computers until I reached cruising altitude, then I turned on the autopilot and sat back to monitor the flight.

It was a relief to talk, even if it was by text, to Grace. She seemed to understand why I hadn't been there to pick her up last night for our date.

Even though she seemed to be understanding, I knew that I still had to make it up to her. With two sisters and two sisters-in-law, I like to think I knew a little bit about the complexities of how women thought. Not that any man could ever really understand.

The most obvious solution was to make my way back to Houston. With the way the schedule was looking, however, there didn't appear to be any chance whatsoever of that anytime soon.

What I needed was an excuse.

There were times when a man had to be careful what he wished for.

When my wheels touched the ground in Philadelphia, my phone began chiming with messages.

A quick glance told me I had a message from Grace.

I smiled to myself as I taxied across the tarmac to the private plane area. I would find a way to get back to Houston.

I waited to look at the message. I waited until after I'd secured the airplane and gone through the post flight checklist.

My passenger would be here in less than an hour so I had time to go into the terminal. Get a coffee.

I saved Grace's message until after I had my cup of coffee in hand and was seated at a little table. I wanted to give her my undivided attention.

A couple with a large white Husky in tow came into the terminal. Not my client. Anytime we had a pet fly with us, we knew it ahead of time.

I didn't mind the pets and this one sat quietly—well behaved. I didn't mind the pets at all.

I unlocked my phone and opened up my text messages with anticipation.

It was time to talk to Grace.

> **GRACE**
>
> Jonathan didn't come to work today. He had clients. Have you heard from him?

And just like that everything fell apart.

Chapter Twenty-One
GRACE

Not only did Jonathan not show up for his nine o'clock appointment, he didn't show up for his ten or his eleven o'clock either.

I went through the same procedure with each of them. I told them that Jonathan had gotten tied up with an emergency and took their information to reschedule.

It was a lie and I knew it. Any emergency Jonathan might be dealing with was an emergency of his own.

It was unthinkable for him to leave clients hanging like this.

I imagined the worst even as I pushed the thoughts aside.

Just as with Benjamin last night, there had to be a logical explanation.

I just didn't know what it was yet.

It would all make sense soon enough.

After I finished up with my nine o'clock client, I sent Benjamin a text.

I had a response after my ten o'clock.

> **BENJAMIN**
> No. I haven't heard anything from him since I drove him to work yesterday.

> He was at work yesterday.

> **BENJAMIN**
> I'll call his wife.

> I have a session now, but I'll check in afterwards.

I put my phone back on silence and got through my next session. It took a lot of work to stay focused on my client when what I wanted to do was to figure out what to do about Jonathan.

As soon as she left my office, I dashed back to my phone.

I had two messages from Benjamin.

> **BENJAMIN**
> She still doesn't answer her phone.

> **BENJAMIN**
> I have a flight now. Talk soon.

> I'm not sure what to do.

He didn't answer, of course. He was still on his flight.

I sat down in my office chair and stared at the vase of roses sitting on my desk.

Something had happened to Jonathan.

Benjamin would know more than I did about what that might be. He knew that Jonathan was going through something.

Maybe he was sick. Maybe he'd had an accident.

He was married. His wife would be with him.

I straightened in my chair, clear now about what I had to do.

I was his work partner.

A work partner had work responsibilities. My responsibility was to his clients until further notice.

I logged into the schedule and began making phone calls.

I cancelled all his afternoon appointments, then after some hesitation, went ahead and cancelled his tomorrow's appointments.

I kept my appointments for tomorrow and since I only had one for this afternoon, I kept it, too.

Just because Jonathan wasn't available didn't mean that my clients should be inconvenienced.

Since I had the time and needed to clear my head, I went downstairs to the bar. They had a good lunch menu and I could use the distraction.

I ordered a shrimp po'boy, then checked my messages.

I had a total of twelve matches now on the dating app. Was this normal? I didn't even know?

Curious, I glanced through them as I responded with disinterested checkmarks.

I was considering deleting the app when a new message from Benjamin came in.

> BENJAMIN
> I'm on my way down there.

> Did you find him?

BENJAMIN

> No. But I have a key to his house. On my way. Talk soon.

This must be bad. Really bad. For Benjamin to drop everything and fly back when he had just flown out last night.

Although I was still worried about Jonathan, my heart was beating a little faster now in anticipation at seeing Benjamin.

I had a client in a couple of hours. Benjamin would probably be here by the time I was out.

At least, hopefully, I would know something soon.

If he had a key, I would know something soon.

Chapter Twenty-Two

BENJAMIN

Less than twenty-four hours after I flew out of Houston, I was back.

The weather was just as hot and muggy as it had been yesterday. Summer in Houston was consistent that way.

After the wheels of my Cessna touched the tarmac in a nice smooth landing, I taxied over toward the private area where a Skye Travels crew stood waiting to take over the airplane.

The Cessna was one of Noah Worthington's airplanes and his crew would service it.

I'd contacted Uncle Noah directly. Explained the situation with my friend. Noah had not hesitated. He'd transferred me to one of his assistants with instructions to "make it happen."

All my flights were scheduled with someone else for the foreseeable future and a flight plan was filed for me to return to Houston.

I would have thought that it was nice to be related to the owner of the company, but that wasn't it.

Uncle Noah was good to his people, even those not related to him. He had no qualms about hiring family members, but like his other employees, the family members who worked for him were the best at what they did.

To say that he was good to his people was an understatement. According to some of the legends I'd heard, he had set up satellite hubs in places like Mackinac Island and Whiskey Springs, Colorado simply because he had pilots who wanted to relocate there. Of course as with everything Noah touched, those hubs had been good business decisions. I had no doubt that he knew that before he did agreed to set them up.

But failure was not in Noah's vocabulary.

Noah's assistant had arranged to have a chauffeured car waiting for me at the airport so I didn't have to worry about renting one or hiring an Uber.

The chauffeur, Peter, looked at me in the rearview mirror.

"Where to Mr. Ashton?"

"Head toward Uptown. Let me check."

In the backseat of the car, I sent Grace a message.

> Are you still at the office?

A couple of minutes later she wrote back.

> **GRACE**
> Yes. Finishing up some charting.

> I'll pick you up in about

I checked my watch.

> 45 minutes

Thought bubbles.

> **GRACE**
> Pick me up? Aren't you going to Jonathan's house?

> You're on the way.

Thought bubbles.
Then no response.

If I hadn't been so worried about Jonathan, I would been amused.

Grace seemed so surprised that I would want to take her with me to look for Jonathan.

In all truthfulness, it probably wasn't the best of ideas, but I couldn't resist the excuse to spend time with her even if it was just going in search of my best friend.

About ten minutes out from her office, she wrote back.

> **GRACE**
> I'll be in the lobby.

Now I did smile. It had taken her a few minutes to work it out, but she did.

Chapter Twenty-Three
GRACE

I stood next to a tall indoor tree in the lobby of my building. There was a lady, probably in her mid-thirties, pulling a watering wagon along behind her to water the plants using a wand.

Other than her, there was no one else around.

I watched the traffic outside, waiting for Benjamin to pull up. It was too hot to stand outside and wait.

A sleek black sedan pulled up outside the door and someone got out of the backseat.

At first I didn't pay the car much attention, but then I realized that Benjamin was the man who stepped out of the backseat and he was walking toward the door.

He stepped inside the building and slid off his sunglasses.

Since I was the only person in sight, he spotted me right away

"Hi," he said.

"Hi."

For a moment I forgot why he was here. For just a moment I imagined he was here just to see me.

But then I remembered that he was here so that we could find Jonathan.

"Ready?" he asked, obviously not forgetting why he was here.

"Yes."

"Can I take your bag?"

"Sure." I handed him my laptop bag and we walked together out to the waiting car.

The driver, dressed in a black tuxedo, got out, took my bag from Benjamin and stashed it in the trunk before he opened the back door.

"Grace," Benjamin said. "This is Peter."

"Hi Peter," I said. "It's a pleasure to meet you."

"Likewise," Peter said, holding out his hand.

With a quick glance at Benjamin, I put my hand in his and he assisted me into the backseat.

Benjamin came around and slid in the other side to sit next to me.

"You haven't heard anything from Jonathan?" I asked as Peter pulled out onto the road.

"His phone goes to voicemail. His wife's phone gone to voicemail." He ran a worried hand through his hair.

"You were already worried about him," I said.

"When you met us in the bar, he was telling me that Tiffany had left him."

"Oh." Wow. I was not expecting that. "That's why he was drinking."

"Yes. That's why."

"I see why you were worried about him." I chewed my bottom lip as Peter merged onto the freeway.

"I tried to call her yesterday. To talk to her, but she didn't answer."

"Has he ever disappeared like this before?"

"Not that I know of."

Now I was even more worried than I had been before. As far as I knew, Jonathan didn't struggle with depression, but with his wife leaving him, I didn't know.

Peter pulled into Jonathan's driveway and got out to open my door. A black iron gate blocked us from driving any further.

"Thank you, Peter," Benjamin said.

"My pleasure. I'll be waiting right here."

I had never been to Jonathan's house. It wasn't anything like I had expected, but then I hadn't really known what to expect.

It was a large two-story white brick house with two dormers on what looked like the third floor.

The lawn was neatly manicured. Very tidy. One large oak tree to shade the front of the house.

A matching brick wall surrounded the house leaving just the driveway open.

From the looks of the house, Jonathan was doing well for himself.

Benjamin got out and motioned for me to follow him toward the front door.

The front door, in contrast to the rest of the house, was painted in black with glass windows above it.

The house, in what I thought of as a New England design, had no front porch or stoop.

Benjamin put the key in the lock and opened up the door.

"After you," he said.

I wasn't sure I wanted to go in first, but I did.

The house opened up into a large open living room with a big comfortable sectional. All the furniture had white upholstery with throw pillows used for accent.

His wife—I assumed it was his wife—had a good eye for color and décor.

I stood just inside the door and waited for Benjamin.

A fluffy cat came running up to him, tail held high, meowing as he ran.

Benjamin bent over and picked him up.

"Hey Charlie. Where's your Daddy?"

Then we heard someone calling out.

"Benjamin. Benjamin. Is that you?"

Benjamin set the cat down and headed through the living room toward the kitchen.

And the stairs.

Jonathan sat on the floor, his back against the wall. His face pale. He was wearing his slacks and a white shirt, obviously ready for work.

"What happened?" Benjamin asked, going to kneel next to him.

"I fell. This morning. Getting ready to go to work."

"I'll get you some water," I said, going to the kitchen and filling a glass with water from the tap.

My hands were shaking.

When I got back, I learned that Jonathan had slipped and fell as he came downstairs.

"Something's broken," he said. "I couldn't move and my phone is upstairs. I was coming down to get a cup of coffee."

Benjamin was on the phone calling the paramedics.

My hands still shaking, I handed him the water.

"Thank you."

"I knew something had to be wrong," I said. "You're always there for your patients."

"My only consolation was knowing you would take care of everything."

"I cancelled everyone from today and tomorrow. Just to be safe."

"Good job," Jonathan said.

"The paramedics are five minutes out," Benjamin said.

"My best friend and my business partner came through for me," Jonathan said, his eyes misting just a little. He was obviously in pain.

"Of course we did," Benjamin said.

"You two make a really great team," he said, then closed his eyes to wait for the paramedics.

Chapter Twenty-Four
BENJAMIN

With Peter driving, Grace and I followed the ambulance to the hospital.

The paramedics seemed to think that Jonathan had dislocated his knee and told us he would be better in no time.

In the meantime, they gave Jonathan some kind of sedative.

It was disconcerting to see Jonathan like this. A reminder for me, at least, that we were nearing thirty years old and we had to start being more careful and taking care of ourselves.

Even Grace seemed to be a little shaken.

"Are you okay?" I asked.

"Relieved, really," she said with a little nod. "I couldn't help but imagine the worst."

"Yeah," I said, "me too."

As Peter pulled into the hospital, I put a hand over Grace's.

"Thank you," I said softly.

"For what?"

"Just for being here. For taking care of everything for Jonathan."

"You don't have to thank me," she said. "It's part of being in business with someone."

"Still," he said. "It was good of you to go out of your way. Good of you to notice, even, that he wasn't there."

"Would you like me to wait, Mr. Ashton?" Peter asked.

"Peter can drive you home," I said.

"If it's all the same," I said. "I'll stay and see this through."

"Sounds good," I said, then answered Peter. "You're fine to wait, but if you have something else you need to do, you can go ahead."

"I don't have anything else," Peter said. "The car is yours for the day. As long as you need it."

"In that case," I said. "I'll keep you posted. Let you know when we're ready."

"Yeah. Just let me know. I won't be far."

Peter got out and opened Grace's door, then drove over to park out of the way.

Grace and I walked toward the hospital doors.

"I'm glad neither one of us said anything to Jonathan about our session," I said. "He doesn't need to worry about us right now."

"Agreed."

We stepped inside the building that smelled of antiseptic. Coming in this back entrance, the hospital looked pretty much deserted.

We sat in the waiting area while Jonathan got checked in and they took him back for an examination.

"Did you ever get in touch with Tiffany?" Grace asked.

"No. But there has to be a logical explanation."

"That's what I keep telling myself about things."

I looked over at her. She was staring straight ahead and I don't know if she was talking about last night or just everything that had happened today.

"I'm sorry about last night."

"It couldn't be helped."

"I should have come by your office before heading up to the airport."

"I doubt you had time," she said, looking at me now with her lovely big green eyes. "You did what you thought you needed to do."

"I did. But it didn't keep me from feeling horrible about standing you up."

"You've got my phone number now," she said.

"Yes. Yes. I do. And it won't happen again."

She smiled, then changed the subject.

"Before all this happened, I'd decided to tell Jonathan about our session."

"I was thinking about telling him, too."

"Maybe tomorrow," she said. "How long are you here?"

"Today at least. Will you let me make it up to you?"

"I'm counting on it."

Chapter Twenty-Five
GRACE

WE STAYED at the hospital for two hours waiting for Jonathan to get checked in and examined.

By then, he was sleeping and wasn't to be disturbed. His nurse, an older woman who brooked no nonsense told us to come back tomorrow.

We both would, of course.

Benjamin texted Peter to pick us up.

"Since we have Peter to drive us around," Benjamin said, where do you want to go?"

"I thought you had everything planned out."

"I did," Benjamin said. "But that was last night. Tonight might be different."

"It might be."

"Do you have a favorite place?"

I shrugged. "I rarely ever get out. I can tell you all about food delivery though if you need to know."

"I'm rather familiar with it myself," he said. "So how do you feel about trying that Italian place I know over in River Oaks?"

"Italian sounds good," I said.

"Then Italian it is."

He held the door for me as we stepped back out into the night air.

"When did it get so late?" I asked.

"It has something to do with the phenomenon of hospitals."

Peter, looking highly professional, was waiting for us at the curb.

Benjamin might be used to such service, but I couldn't say the same.

Moonlight blended with the bright overhead parking lot lights as Benjamin opened the back door of the car for me.

The car, with its buttery soft leather seats, had a new car smell. A clean smell.

Benjamin climbed into the backseat next to me and sat toward the middle.

He gave Peter the name of the restaurant.

"Do you need me to look up the address?" Benjamin asked.

"I've already got it." Peter said. "How is Dr. Baker?"

"He'll be okay. Probably out of the hospital in a couple of days, then he'll be back on his feet in no time."

"That's good news," Peter said.

"We really need that receptionist he keeps talking about," I said. "The scheduling is going to be a nightmare."

"Aren't you an equal partner?"

"I guess so," I said, "but it's Jonathan's company."

"Maybe while he's in the hospital is a good time to hire someone."

"Maybe. But ironically I don't have the time to do interviews, much less train anyone."

"I can ask Un—Noah's wife. She's a psychologist. I'm guessing she can refer someone."

"Maybe it would be okay on a trial basis," I said. "I don't think it's right to make any major life changes while he's out." Besides, I didn't know how I would pay anyone or even what to offer them.

"I think she has a temp agency she's used before," he said. "Let me find out."

He proceeded to type a message to Savannah Worthington.

The fact that Benjamin even had her phone number was a surprise to me. That he felt comfortable enough to text her out of the blue was baffling.

"She'll get back to me," he said.

Peter merged onto the freeway.

"It's a full moon," I said, looking out my window.

Benjamin pushed a button and the top of the car slid back, revealing the sky above us.

"Where?" he asked.

"I don't know if you can see if from your side." But I leaned over and looked up through the sky roof.

"There it is," I said.

Benjamin leaned close so he could see the moon also.

He smelled like a mix of a clean mountain forest with a hint of jet fuel.

With him being so close, my heart skipped into overdrive.

"I see it," he said, so close his breath brushed against my ear.

Just as he went to kiss me on the cheek, I turned and our lips brushed.

Neither one of us moved for what seemed like an eternity but was probably only a few seconds.

The sounds of traffic swirled around us and I could just hear the faint sound of the baseball game Peter was listening to.

Benjamin shifted and his lips pressed against mine.

Then we both moved away.

"I think we're breaking all sorts of ethics," I whispered.

"I'm sure we are," he said. "But. I was thinking."

"What were you thinking?"

"I was wondering if maybe we just didn't tell anyone that I pretended to be your client."

"Pretended."

"Yes. Well. Maybe not pretended. Maybe accidentally."

"I don't know," I said, pressed my fingers against my forehead. "I have to think about it."

Benjamin put his arm around me.

"Maybe you shouldn't think so hard," he said.

"I can't help it."

"I know."

He kissed me again, on the cheek this time.

"I think we're here," he said.

And he was right. The car had stopped moving and I hadn't even realized it.

Looked like I needed to think harder than either one of us could have anticipated.

Chapter Twenty-Six
BENJAMIN

The little Italian restaurant that smelled like deliciously fresh baked bread was quiet with just a hint of music playing in the background.

It wasn't crowded. In fact there were only two other couples at tables scattered around the smallish restaurant.

All in all, I'd say I'd made a good choice.

It met all the requirements I'd been looking for. White tables cloths. Live flowers—white daisies—in little glass vases in the middle of each table.

The server brought a bottle of champagne and after pouring some into a flute for each of us, burrowed it into a bucket of ice on the table.

"This is nice," Grace said.

"I thought you might like it," I said. "You don't get out nearly enough."

She looked at me sideways. "I told you that, didn't I?"

"I think you did."

"I'm just glad Jonathan is okay. I was really worried about him."

"You're a good friend."

The server stopped by and took our order, then went on his way.

"Did you ever find out why Tiffany left him?"

"Not yet," I said. "But I will."

"You sound so certain about that."

"I was his best man at his wedding. It's my responsibility."

She smiled as she sipped her champagne.

"I'm not so sure it works like that. It would be nice if it did."

"Oh. It will. I warned them both that he worked too much."

"Did you now?"

"I did. And they both promised that they understood and that they were okay with it."

"Things change, you know." She said, breaking off a piece of a long skinny breadstick.

"What happened to you turning everything into a positive?"

"Sometimes I have to temper my positivity with a healthy dose of reality."

"I see."

"Yeah. I don't care for it either. But people get tired of everything being spun in a positive direction."

"I don't."

"Then you're the exception."

I grinned. "I'm the exception to a lot of things."

"Incorrigible," she said, mostly to herself, but it brought a grin to my face.

She was right. I was feeling quite incorrigible at the moment if being incorrigible meant wanting to kiss her again.

I liked everything about her. Her red bow shaped lips that turned up at the corners even when she was trying not to smile.

Long flowing brunette hair that swirled around her shoulders.

And even more, her big green eyes with long dark lashes that seemed to see right into the very deep recesses of my thoughts.

Maybe it was the psychologist in her. Or maybe it was just those eyes.

Whatever it was, she had me turned inside out.

"You look deep in thought," she said.

I smiled into her eyes.

"I was just thinking."

"I think there's something we need to talk about," she said.

"You do know that those four words *We need to talk* strike fear into the heart of every man."

She tried not to smile, but her eyes glowed with amusement.

"Maybe there's a reason for that."

"Probably. What is it we need to talk about?"

She swirled the bubbly champagne in her glass and took a little sip.

"You said you pretended to be a client."

"I did say that, didn't I?

She nodded and lifted one delicate brow.

"I wasn't pretending. Exactly. Maybe a little. But it wasn't on purpose."

She looked at me with narrowed eyes.

"I didn't know that Jonathan had moved his office."

"I thought as much."

"And you just pulled me right in. How was I supposed to resist?"

Lowering her eyes, she looked into her champagne flute.

"You have a good point," she said. "And you're right. I did just pull you right in. I thought you were my client. A new client scheduled at that time."

She pushed her hair back away from her face and let it fall down her back.

"The timing couldn't have been better if you had done it intentionally."

"I was planning to catch Jonathan in between clients, but I was running a little late."

"That makes sense."

"And then on top of being charmed, I was curious."

"Curious about what?"

I shook my head. "Just curious. About you. About the questions you were asking. It was sort of like being on a date, but cutting to the chase."

"I don't understand."

"It felt like we were getting all the basic questions out of the way without the games."

"But it wasn't a date."

"I know. And I'm sorry about that."

"You wanted it to be a date."

And now it felt like a session.

"I guess I sort of did want it to be date. It felt like we were being so candid with each other. Or I was anyway. I liked that. I honestly forgot that it was supposed to be a session. It felt like we were just getting to know each other."

We'd had a session that felt like a date and now a date that felt like a session.

Chapter Twenty-Seven
GRACE

While we sat in the little restaurant, a pianist sat down and started playing music on the grand piano that sat across the room.

We were far enough away that the music faded into the background along with the conversations that swirled around us.

There weren't many other customers when we first came in, but now it was starting to fill up. People seemed to know when the live music started and showed up for that if nothing else.

Benjamin, sitting across from me at the table covered with a white cloth and a glass vase with a live daisy in it, looked rather decidedly guilty.

I was making him sweat and I knew it.

He confirmed what I had already figured out. He'd come to my office looking for Jonathan, but instead had found me.

I had ushered him in and started doing my standard intake. Granted, I had deviated from my usual questions quite a bit. Maybe my instinct had told me that he wasn't really there for a session or maybe deep down I knew I was going to have to refer him to someone else.

I'd kept the intake questions light and I'd enjoyed talking to him.

So maybe he was right. Maybe it hadn't really been a session.

I could easily spin it in my head so that it wasn't.

But it was.

It had been a session at the time. It was just in retrospect, neither one of us wanted it to be.

What was I supposed to do with that?

I wasn't going to be able to figure it out by myself. Not now.

It was like beating my head against a wall.

The only way I was going to sort this out was to consult with another psychologist. Maybe not Jonathan. Maybe I would find someone else to consult with. Maybe someone I didn't work with.

I couldn't be mad at Benjamin. I was as much at fault as he was. Actually I was more at fault. I was the psychologist. I knew better.

He was simply a client.

Apparently I was going to drive myself around in circles over this until it was sorted out.

Another reason why I needed to consult with someone on the best way to resolve it.

An added problem was that he had gone and kissed me.

I'd not only let him, I had liked it.

And not only that, but I wanted him to do it again.

The whole thing was a slippery slope. Now that he had kissed me, I didn't see any way to go back.

There wasn't a way to go back.

We could only go forward.

I was finding it hard to think with him looking at me with those deep blue eyes. Eyes that didn't seem to see anything other than me.

"I'll be right back," I said, putting my cloth napkin on the table in front of me.

Maybe I just needed a minute... a walk to the restroom and back... to clear my head.

Chapter Twenty-Eight
BENJAMIN

I watched Grace walk through what was now a crowded restaurant toward the restrooms.

Sitting back, I studied the other people in the room. Most of the other diners were couples, like Grace and I were.

We might not actually be a couple, but we looked like a couple and we were acting like a couple.

If it walked like a duck and it quacked like a duck, it was safe to call it a duck.

Thank you Jonathan for that profound insight.

The piano music was pleasant and relaxing. It was almost like being at an orchestra of one.

The pianist wasn't any older than I was, but he could play the piano like a professional.

I recognized a familiar chime on my phone. It was a dating app I'd used a couple of times. I hadn't expected to actually meet anyone through the app, but I found it an entertaining way to pass some of the time I spent waiting at airports.

I checked my phone, intending to silence it, but it was already on silent and I didn't have any notifications on the app.

Carefully picking up Grace's discarded cloth napkin, I found the phone she had left on the table.

I didn't mean to pry, but it was right there.

She was the one getting a notification through the app.

She had a new match.

Well. It hadn't occurred to me that she might be dating others.

But, of course, it made sense that she would be.

She was an attractive, successful woman. One men would be attracted to.

And another peak at her phone told me that she had fourteen matches. The new one was number fourteen.

Fourteen.

I'd gotten three in as many months that I'd toyed with it. I hadn't actually gone out with any of the girls I was matched with. I wasn't a big fan of dating apps.

I liked to meet my girls the old-fashioned way.

Like walking into their offices and letting them ask me anything they wanted to ask about my life.

Very efficient.

But Grace, on the other hand, seemed to be having quite a popularity spurt on the app.

I wondered how long she had been on it.

My guess was not very long because she didn't seem to know how to clear off the unwanted matches.

Unless, of course, she was wanting to come back to them.

Feeling like I had intruded on her privacy, I dropped the napkin back over her phone before she came back.

I was not in the habit of invading others' privacy and I hadn't intended to start with Grace.

I was, however, more than happy to talk with her about anything if she wanted to.

Minutes later, she came back to the table.

I watched her carefully as she put her napkin back in her lap, then looked at her phone.

Instead of being delighted, she scowled at the new match.

I took that as a good sign that, like me, she wasn't very interested in the app.

She dropped her phone into her purse and turned her attention to me.

"I think we need to set some ground rules," she said.

I put my arms on the table and leaned forward. "I'm all for ground rules. Let's hear it."

"Okay." She mirrored my pose, her arms on the table and cleared her throat.

"I think we need to meet with someone, another psychologist, to help us sort through this."

"Couples therapy. That sounds fun."

"No," she said with obvious exasperation. "Not couples therapy."

I hid a smile.

"What then?"

"It's called a consult. When a psychologist has a question about something, the first thing they're supposed to do is consult with a colleague."

"Okay. Like Jonathan."

"Yes. Like Jonathan. But I'm not sure Jonathan is the best one for us since we're both close to him."

Now she was making me a little nervous. I knew and trusted Jonathan. And I knew and trusted Grace. Other psychologists, not so much.

Another psychologist was likely to tell us to never see each other again. They might not understand.

And unless I was reading Grace all wrong, she would abide by whatever this consult said.

"Okay," I said again. "I'm willing to do this on one condition."

"What's that?"

"I'm willing to do this consulting thing if we can at least start with Jonathan. If he can't resolve it, then we'll go to someone else."

She hesitated. Took a sip of her champagne.

"Okay," she said finally. "We'll start with Jonathan."

"Good," I sat back, feeling rather smug.

"But," Grace said. "In the meantime, we have to have ground rules."

"Right. The ground rules. How many?"

"I'm still working on that. So far I have one."

I knew what she was going to say before she said it.

"No kissing."

"I'm no longer a fan of ground rules."

She smiled then, before she caught herself.

"I think if we can do that, we can figure the rest out as we go."

I couldn't help thinking about ways around this rule, but if it was important to her, then who was I was to say that it wasn't important?

"Okay," I said. "We have our ground rules. Or rather one ground rule. Now what?"

"Now we eat," she said as the server set our plates in front of us.

I didn't even remember us ordering.

Grace had me that thrown off balance.

The good news was I couldn't think of anyone I'd rather be off balance with.

Chapter Twenty-Nine

GRACE

The piano player changed from one song to another, moving into a romantic song that I had a personal affinity for. The song about love lost and found again had always resonated with me. It might be the words or it might just be the catchy melody. Probably a little bit of both.

We didn't talk about anything much while we ate. It felt all in all quite comfortable being here with him.

My no kissing rule came at a cost.

Benjamin took it in stride.

In fact, he seemed to take it better than us meeting with a consultant. I could, of course, meet with the consultant by myself. That's how it was typically done anyway.

After all, he was the client and I had to do what was in his best interest.

The problem was that I wanted to kiss him again. All night long wouldn't be long enough.

But it seemed very important that we not continue to slide down that slippery slope.

Not, at least, without consulting with another psychologist.

I had worked for too many years to get my license to practice psychology to have it taken away for any reason.

I suppose, though, that if there had to be a reason, any reason at all, he would be a good one. He was incredibly handsome with his five o'clock shadow. With the hint of a dimple when he smiled. And those eyes. Blue eyes that latched onto mine and held.

He caught me looking at him and winked.

I quickly looked away, but I felt the sting of heat creeping up my cheeks.

"Since you know all about me, am I allowed to ask you something personal?" he asked.

"Of course," I said, setting my fork down. "You can ask."

"I should have already asked you this. Are you dating anyone?"

"I haven't had time to date anyone in forever."

"So no boyfriend?"

"No boyfriend." I thought about the dating app and the influx of matches I'd already gotten. They didn't interest me.

The only match who interested me right now was sitting here at the table with me.

"Why not?"

"Why not what?"

"Why don't you have a boyfriend?"

"No time," I said.

He looked at me sideways.

"We both know that we make time for things that are important to us."

I swirled the bubbly champagne in my glass. Watched as the light reflected off the bubbles.

"You're right. But since clients aren't a dating pool, that doesn't leave much time for finding someone to date."

"Huh." He shoved his plate aside and leaned his elbows on the table, locking his eyes on mine again.

"Huh what?" I asked, biting my lip to keep from smiling.

"Nothing," he said. "I'm just thinking how funny it is that I ended up in your office."

"It is rather odd, isn't it? Did you ever talk to Tiffany?"

"No," he said, falling for my change of subject. "I need to call her, actually, and tell her that Jonathan is in the hospital."

"Right. I didn't think to do that either."

"Maybe it'll be enough to get them talking again."

"I hope so." If Benjamin and I were going to talk to Jonathan about dating/not dating, then it would be helpful if his own relationship was going in a good direction again.

"You have clients in the morning?" he asked.

"Yes. Starting early."

"I'm planning to stick around until either Jonathan gets out of the hospital or Tiffany comes back."

"I think that's a good idea," I said. "I think it's important that he has a friend with him."

"I agree."

"He doesn't seem clumsy," I said, thinking about how he could have fallen.

"No. But there's one thing I've learned about that. Stairs can be tricky for anyone."

"I guess so." I sat back and ran a finger along the moisture on my glass. "It's scary to think about."

"You think too much."

"So you've said."

He grinned, giving me a quick glimpse of his dimple.

"Do you want to get out of here? Take a walk?"

"A walk? Where?"

"I don't know," he said, holding up a hand for the check. "I'm sure we can think of something."

Chapter Thirty
BENJAMIN

At Peter's recommendation, we ended up at the Waterwall Park since it wasn't far from the restaurant.

He parked the car not far from the Transco Tower and waited for us there while we walked in the moonlight beneath the oak trees.

"I've driven by here a hundred times," I said. "But I've never gotten out and walked it."

"It's hard to imagine that there are more than one hundred oak trees right here within walking distance of the Galleria."

"I thought it was the Transco Tower," I mentioned. "But according to the sign back there it's the William's Tower."

"It's one of those things about being a true Houstonian. Houstonians all know it's the Transco Tower."

"So they changed the name?"

"Officially," she said. "But it'll always be the Transco Tower."

"Good to know," I said.

The waterfall in a semicircle ahead of us glowed with golden lights and the roar of water falling over sixty feet growing louder as we neared.

We were one of only half a dozen people out walking in the park tonight.

As we entered the semicircle, I took Grace's hand.

Standing together, we looked up at the architectural wonder, a little spray of water hitting our faces.

"This is nice," he said. "I bet it's even tolerably cool enough right here in the daytime."

"It might be," I said, looking up at him.

Squeezing my hand, he pulled me closer and slowly lowered his head.

My eyes fluttered closed as I anticipated his kiss.

As his lips neared mine, I sighed.

Then he kissed me on the cheek.

"I'm sorry," he said. "I almost forgot our ground rule."

"Our ground—" I mentally kicked myself. "Right."

Here at this fountain was the perfect place for a kiss. The light spray of water on our faces. The light of the moon a backdrop to the waterfall lit with golden lights.

It was magical.

"I think maybe we should consider a temporary suspension considering the circumstance."

I had no more than gotten the words out than his lips were on mine.

Maybe we needed something more like a permanent suspension.

He pulled back and looked into my eyes.

"I'd like to propose a change to the ground rule."

"Okay," I said, licking my lips. "To what?"

"I propose that we move the no kissing rule to daytime only."

"Does that mean that night time would be...?"

"Kissing would be allowed at night. But only at night."

I nodded. "Considering the circumstances, I second that change."

"It's official then," he said. "Kissing is allowed at night."

Then he kissed me again, stopping only when a group of people walked near us.

"I should get you home," he said.

"Right. Of course."

My brain had turned to mush.

It had been the perfect kiss in a magical setting.

Chapter Thirty-One
GRACE

Sitting close to me, Benjamin held my hand on the drive back to my townhouse.

My lips still tingled from that kiss beneath the waterfall.

My clothes were slightly damp, but I didn't care.

Benjamin, also with slightly damp clothes, smelled like fresh air.

Since Peter parked the car in visitor parking and waited there, we had to walk a few yards to my front door.

Benjamin opened my little gate and walked with me to my front door.

"Thank you," he said, pressing a hand against the door casing.

"For what?"

"For a lovely evening. Everything considered."

"I should be the one thanking you."

"Maybe we should thank Jonathan."

"It is rather his fault," I said.

Benjamin laughed and pressed his other hand on the other side of my door.

My door was in shadows. A lot of my neighbors had automatic lights that turned on when someone walked up, but my unit didn't have one and since I usually went in through the garage, I had never worried about it.

"It's still nighttime," Benjamin said.

"I know."

He pulled me close, wrapping his arms around me.

I melted against him, the door at my back, and his arms catching me.

He kissed me thoroughly this time, taking his time.

Somewhere in the back of my mind, I knew that Peter was waiting for him.

Then the thought drifted away along with any other vaguely coherent thoughts that wandered through my head.

He had me pressed against him, the door at my back. Our bodies were pressed together, but he had me focused on what he was doing with his lips and his tongue.

I felt like my whole body was on fire and I couldn't get close enough to him.

Then something happened so suddenly and so unexpectedly that I was caught completely off guard.

As I reached a peak and tumbled over, he caught my gasp with his mouth against mine.

I would have fallen to the ground if his arms hadn't kept me upright.

He kissed me until I floated back to earth, then he kissed my eyelids and my nose before leaning back enough that he could look at me.

I forced my eyes open and dreaded meeting his gaze. I dreaded what I would see in his eyes. What would he think of me? So easily seduced.

But he gently swept a lock of hair off my face.

"You're beautiful," he said.

I saw no judgement. No laughter. Just emotion.

"Keys?" he asked.

I somehow managed to dig my keys out of my purse while still holding onto his arm with one hand.

When he held out his hand, I gave him my keys and waited while he unlocked the door.

"Goodnight, my sweet," he said, kissing me again, lightly on the lips.

"Goodnight."

He opened my door and after I stepped inside, he closed the door behind me.

After throwing the lock, I walked on wobbly legs to my sofa and sat down.

Oh. My. God.

Benjamin had barely touched me and I had climaxed mostly from his kiss. Maybe a little with being pressed against him. Maybe a lot from being pressed against him. Maybe both.

I'd thought I would be embarrassed, but Benjamin had been a gentleman and had pretended not to notice that he had exploded my world.

He'd looked at me with compassion and care that left me not the least bit embarrassed.

Instead, I was confused.

He and I had made a deal that we would only kiss at night—a ridiculously flimsy ground rule if ever there was one.

A ground rule established in the heat of the moment.

A moment I would cherish for eternity and one I would never forget.

I had fallen right down that slippery slope and hit the ground solidly and irrefutably in love.

Chapter Thirty-Two
BENJAMIN

With Peter easily navigating evening traffic, I made my way back to Jonathan's house.

If Tiffany was home, I would leave and get a hotel. I considered doing that anyway, but someone had to feed the cat and spend some time with the little guy.

Settled on Jonathan's sofa, Charlie jumped into my lap, started purring, and rubbing his face against my hands.

After the cat settled down, lying on my chest, I kicked off my shoes and stretched out on the sofa.

I'd meant it when I'd said Grace and I needed to thank Jonathan for our evening.

He was the reason I'd come back to Houston and he was the reason I'd gotten to spend a magical evening with Grace.

Dinner had been lovely. Our walk in Waterwall Park had been romantic.

But kissing her goodnight had been a one of a kind experience.

There was something innocent about Grace.

Even though she had responded to my kisses in a most intimate way, I was certain that she didn't have a lot of experience.

I liked that. I liked it a lot.

Hell. I liked everything about her.

I liked the way her hair fell around her shoulders when she didn't pull it back.

I like the way she bit her bottom lip to try to keep from smiling.

I liked it that she had shown me complete trust while I kissed her.

There was nothing innocent about me. That didn't mean that I couldn't appreciate it in her.

In fact, I allowed myself to indulge in a double standard. As a man I was supposed to have more experience than she did. Just ask any man.

The fact that she had that dating app bothered me.

And the fact that it bothered me and that I actually wanted to protect her from whoever she might meet on that app or anywhere else for that matter told me a lot. It told me that I had finally met the girl who had the ability to turn my world upside down.

I just had to get her past this whole client problem.

In my opinion we had made great strides today in getting rid of it.

When I heard the garage door open, I automatically slid my feet off the couch and sat up. Charlie jumped down and headed toward the back door.

It could only be one person. Charlie might be looking for Jonathan, but I knew it could only be Tiffany.

I followed the cat to the kitchen so that Tiffany would see me when she stepped through the door.

"Jonathan said you would be here," Tiffany said as she scooped up the cat.

Tiffany was model thin. Long blonde hair. She usually had a smile ready on her lips, but not tonight. Tonight she looked tired.

"I can go. Get a room somewhere."

"Don't be ridiculous." She set the cat down and moved to fill his food bowl even though I'd filled it less than an hour ago.

"You know you always have a place to stay here."

I put my hands in my pockets.

"Are you okay? Jonathan was worried about you. And upset."

"We had a disagreement," she said with a wave of her head that told me she didn't want to talk about it.

"Must have been serious," I said. I honestly didn't care if she told me or not. I just didn't like the state she'd left Jonathan in.

Straightening, she looked at me.

"You're a good friend."

"He's a good man."

She dropped onto the nearest bar stool and sighed. Charlie rubbed against her and she absently picked him up.

Personally, I don't think she could have left the cat permanently. Charlie was her cat, after all.

"We're fine," she said. "We worked it out. Thank you for being here when he needed someone."

"You don't have to thank me," I said. "Jonathan and I have been taking care of each other for a really long time."

"Mates before dates," she said with a little tired smile.

I grinned. "Something like that. Mind if I get a bottle of water?"

"You know your way around."

"You want one?"

"Sure."

I took two bottles of water out of the refrigerator, twisted the lid on one and handed it to her.

Not drinking it, she set it on the bar.

"So tell me about Grace," she said.

"Grace? What about her?" I leaned against the table behind me. I wasn't prepared to talk about Grace. She and I had a lot of things to work out before we talked to anyone else, no matter what Grace kept saying about consultants.

"Nothing. Jonathan seems to think that the two of you seem to have hit it off."

"Jonathan doesn't miss anything, does he?"

"Not really. It's one of the downsides of being married to a psychologist."

"And being friends with one."

"I met Grace. She seems like a nice girl. Jonathan says she's one of the best psychologists he's worked with."

"I wouldn't know about that," I said, not even going near the whole psychologist thing. "But I agree. She's... smart and funny and kind."

"Jonathan was right," Tiffany said with that same tired little smile. She was worried about Jonathan. I could tell. "You are taken with her."

"What can I say?" I shrugged.

"A gentleman never kisses and tells."

I didn't know what was going on between Jonathan and Tiffany, but Tiffany was smart. As far as I was concerned, Jonathan had married well.

Seems he had excellent taste in women. Both personally and professionally.

Chapter Thirty-Three

GRACE

The next day I hit the ground running.

I not only had a busy day of clients, but I fielded emails and website messages as I rescheduled Jonathan's clients.

I'd spoken to him briefly. Just long enough to determine that he would be taking a week off to recover enough to come back to work. As far as I knew this was the first time he had ever missed work.

In between clients, when I sat with my door open, busily charting sessions and answering emails, I kept an eye on the door.

Benjamin said he would be staying until Jonathan got back on his feet—literally—or Tiffany returned.

Since Jonathan hadn't said anything about Tiffany, I had to assume she wasn't back. And from there I assumed that Benjamin was still around.

I hoped he would let me know before he left this time. He had my number, but I hadn't heard anything from him.

No text. No call. And he hadn't shown up here at the office.

I caught myself fretting over him.

Maybe I had read too much into our date last night.

Just because he had rocked my world, didn't mean that the feeling was mutual.

It was possible that I had moved too fast for him. That I had been too easy. It wasn't like we had slept together.

We had just sort of made out. It was what people did.

People went on dates and they made out.

I refused to feel bad about it.

I was a normal red-blooded girl and Benjamin was a very attractive red-blooded boy.

My logic warred with my emotions as I prepared for my next client.

It was my late night to work.

I added some water to my vase of roses and took a moment to run my fingers over the soft petals that were starting to open up a bit.

My phone chimed with another message on the dating app.

While I waited for my client to show up, I sat down at my desk thinking I would just delete the app altogether.

I had a new match. This made seventeen. I only knew because the app kept track.

With a sudden burst of curiosity, I changed my parameters. I changed my location from Houston to Pittsburgh.

I was looking for a handsome pilot named Benjamin Ashton.

But I didn't see him on the app.

Irritated with myself, I deleted the app. I didn't want it anymore.

There. With the app gone, I didn't have to worry about that anymore.

Even if I never saw Benjamin again, it would be okay. I could safely say that I had a better idea of what kind of man I liked.

As I waited for my seven o'clock client, the sun started its descent over the horizon.

I had a newly acquired affinity for nighttime.

Nighttime was when kisses were allowed.

I was being ridiculous. Next thing I'd be writing Mrs. Benjamin Ashton on paper with little hearts.

My client showed up, saving me from myself.

She was a long-standing client and I knew her well. She'd had to switch to nights this month because as a nurse, she'd taken a new job that came with new hours.

She had the usual relationship problems. Almost all the clients I saw had some kind of problem with relationships. Even the married ones.

One client in particular had a great marriage. Loved his wife. But her father lived with them. It put a strain on them. He didn't even want anything to change. He just needed to talk to me now and then to get confirmation that he wasn't insane and he wasn't alone in some of the things he was dealing with.

After my client left, I decided to do her charting from home. It was late and I didn't feel like being at the office any longer.

I grabbed my purse, logged off my computer, and locked up.

As I left my office, I saw Benjamin standing across the hall.

"Hi," he said, smiling.

"Hi. What are you doing?"

My first thought was that he wanted to talk to me as a psychologist.

Sometimes people did that. They just showed up without an appointment.

"Can I walk you to your car?" he asked.

"Okay." I got my feet moving again as I corrected my thoughts.

He wasn't here for a session. He was just here to see me.

He was not a client.

As we walked together toward the elevator, I acknowledged the shift in my thinking.

Despite my initial reaction to seeing him, I wasn't thinking of him as a client anymore.

It would be so easy to rewrite our history.

He had stopped by looking for Jonathan and found me instead. We'd talked. We'd discovered we had mutual interests even though he lived in Pittsburgh.

But pilots saw the world differently from the rest of us. For pilots, the world, or rather the country anyway, was a lot smaller.

Being able to jump on an airplane and be in another city in another state in the same amount of time it sometimes took to drive across Houston changed one's perspective.

I'd worked with another pilot once when I was on my internship and I'd learned a lot about how he saw the world.

"Penny for your thoughts," Benjamin said as we stepped onto the empty elevator.

"Nothing in particular," I said. "Just wrapping up my day of clients in my head."

"It's good that you can compartmentalize your clients from your personal life."

"I had a professor in grad school who taught us how to do that. It's not something that necessarily comes naturally.

"I never gave that much thought," he said. "I don't think pilots do that. We're always thinking about flying."

I smiled. "So I've heard. I didn't say I wasn't thinking about psychology, though. Just tucking other people's problems aside for now."

"Don't I know that," Benjamin said as we stepped off the elevator. "I don't think Jonathan has too many thoughts without his psychology filter on."

"That's an interesting way of putting it."

"He's the one who came up with it. I'm not sure if he does it with Tiffany or not though."

"Oh. Did you ever talk to her?"

"She already knew. I think he called her or someone from the hospital did."

"So… what does that mean?" I wasn't sure what I was asking and he didn't really answer.

"Peter's waiting for us."

"You got Peter to drive you again?"

"To drive us. I like being able to give you all my attention instead of focusing on the traffic."

He opened the back door and I climbed inside.

"Good evening, Dr. Miller," Peter said.

"Good evening, Peter."

As Benjamin slid in on the other side, I considered how easy it would be to get used to being chauffeured around all the time.

Too easy. It would be too easy.

"To answer your question," Benjamin said. "Tiffany is back home and she stayed with Jonathan all day today."

"So they worked everything out?"

"It seems so. I still don't know what it was."

"Something between them," I said. "Not our business."

I couldn't help but wonder what Benjamin had been doing all day.

What could he possibly have been doing? Had he stayed at the hospital, too?

It didn't seem like something appropriate to ask. It seemed like one of those things he would tell me if he wanted me to know. It wasn't really my business after all.

"How was your day?" he asked.

It took me a minute to think about how to answer that question. I couldn't even remember the last time anyone had asked me about my day.

"It was... uneventful."

Benjamin laughed.

"What's funny?"

"It's what pilots say when they had a good flight. An uneventful flight is always considered a good flight."

"I can see that."

Benjamin was wearing his pilot's uniform tonight.

"I had an uneventful day, too. I had to fly someone up to Dallas. Took most of the day to go there and back."

"I see." Relief spread through me.

He'd been working.

I'd worried about what he'd been doing for nothing.

"Where do you want to eat?" he asked.

I leaned back against the seat. I'd been fretting about him all day long. Wondering why he didn't call me or text me or show up.

Now I felt ridiculous. He'd been working. I really needed to use some of my own techniques on myself to keep myself from fretting so much.

I hadn't found any particular technique, though, that worked just yet, but there had to be something out there that would work. I'd keep looking and trying different things.

Chapter Thirty-Four
BENJAMIN

Despite the heat, it was a beautiful night in Houston. The full moon glowed through the sunroof, blending with the street lights as we headed downtown.

"Anyplace in particular you'd like to eat?" I asked.

Grace looked over at me with her big green eyes.

"I don't usually eat when I work late. It looks like we're headed downtown."

"Just driving around," I said. "But there's a little seafood place downtown that comes highly recommended if you like seafood."

"I love seafood."

"Then we'll go there." I leaned forward to speak to Peter. "Can you take us to that seafood place you recommended?"

"We'll be there in thirty-five minutes," Peter said without a moment's hesitation.

I sat back.

"Peter is one of the best chauffeurs I've met."

"I can see that. Do you have a chauffeur at home?"

"Nope. I have a Maserati."

"A sports car?"

"No. Just a car."

"Huh."

I was always curious what psychologists were thinking when they did that. Jonathan said *huh* all the time. I decided to ask her.

"What does it mean when a psychologist says huh?"

"It can mean a lot of things. It can mean surprise. Or agreement. Or maybe we think you're crazy." She smiled. "Usually it just means we don't know what to say right then but we want you to know that we heard you."

"Huh."

She laughed. "That was very good."

"I know."

I reached over and took her hand not just because it seemed like the right thing to do, but because it was something I'd been wanting to do.

We rode in silence until Peter pulled into the restaurant parking lot.

I was content to simply ride in the car holding Grace's hand.

Soon I would be heading back to Pittsburgh and right now I wasn't looking forward to it.

Unfortunately a man had to work for a living. My parents might be well off, but my mother had instilled an ironclad work ethic in all of her children at very early ages.

Not working was not even an option for any of her five children, myself included.

"I'll be here," Peter said. "Just text me when you're ready to go."

"Will do. You don't have to get out."

I went around and opened Grace's door. Held out a hand to help her out of the car.

As we walked toward the little restaurant, I tucked her hand in the crook of my elbow.

"Have you been here before?" I asked.

The parking lot was full of cars. Always a good sign. The restaurant itself was tucked in between two tall office buildings.

The front of the building was lit up with festive twinkly lights that reminded me of the holidays. Peter had assured me that even though it might not be much to look at, the food was excellent. It was a popular place with the Houston Astros.

"I've never even heard of it," she said.

"Me either. But Peter claims it's very popular and has very good food."

"Sounds good to me," she said. "And from the looks of it, Peter is right about it being popular."

"Peter knows things."

"How did you end up with him as a driver?"

This was where things could get tricky. I knew that the sooner I told her the truth, the better it would be. The longer I waited, the worse it would be.

We followed the hostess to a table in the back of the crowded restaurant. Peter was right in that there were a lot of guys who looked like baseball players here.

After we were seated, Grace looked at me with a raised eyebrow.

"It's kind of a long story," I said. Since she wasn't going to be satisfied without a sufficient answer, it seemed like this was about the best time to tell her the truth.

"I've got time," she said, leaning forward on her elbows.

"You know I work for Skye Travels, right?"

"Right. And Peter is one of their drivers."

"He is. Peter was assigned to pick me up at the airport."

"But now he's your personal driver. That seems a bit unusual. Not that I'm complaining."

Sometimes the best way to say something was to just say it outright.

"My grandfather and Noah Worthington are brothers."

She looked blankly at me. Blinked. The usual expression when someone first learned about my grandfather and Noah.

"But he's a Worthington and you're an Ashton."

A server brought us water and offered us glasses of wine.

"That's where the story gets even longer. When they were younger, in their twenties, they had a falling out. It was so bad that my grandfather moved away and changed his name."

"A rather radical decision."

"That's the story they tell us anyway. Probably more to it than that. Anyway, a few years ago, my grandfather had a heart attack and somehow Uncle Noah learned about his brother."

"That must have been strange for everyone."

"It was. It was around the same time I started flying for Skye Travels. It was odd learning that I had an uncle I didn't know about, especially when that uncle is Noah Worthington."

"So Peter works for Noah and... you."

"No. Not me. When I called Noah and asked for help getting

down here to help find Jonathan, he had understood how important it was. He was very helpful and Peter just somehow got thrown into the mix."

"Huh."

"My thoughts exactly."

We both ordered the fried shrimp, a staple around Houston, being near the Gulf of Mexico.

"I should have already told you," I said. "I have to apologize for that."

"You don't have to apologize. You've had a lot going on."

Grace was very understanding. I could get used to being with someone who didn't make a big deal out of things that weren't all that important.

Chapter Thirty-Five
GRACE

The seafood restaurant was, on the surface at least, what most people would call a dive.

But it was packed. Benjamin and I had gotten the last table and now there was a line to get in.

Music played from an old jukebox sitting in one corner. Apparently it didn't require quarters. Just for someone to go over and push the buttons.

Even though I had grown up in Houston, I'd only been downtown a couple of times.

It wasn't what I had expected. It was urban and upscale from what I'd seen so far.

Again, not at all what I had expected.

"There's a place similar to this on the river in Pittsburgh," Benjamin said. "But the food isn't as good. I'll take you there sometime."

My brain had a little glitch at his words. He wanted to take me to Pittsburgh. To a restaurant he knew.

Maybe he was just making conversation.

People did that sometimes.

So I didn't answer. I just smiled at him.

The server stopped by and picked up our plates, cleaned off our table.

The music changed over to something hauntingly and quietly romantic.

Benjamin leaned forward on the table and looked at me.

"It's nighttime," he said.

"It is," I agreed, my calm expression nothing like the rapid beating of my heart.

He leaned forward and kissed me on the lips.

A public display of affection from the most handsome man in the building.

"So can I ask you something?" he asked.

"Sure."

"I accidentally noticed that you have a dating app on your phone."

I was getting the distinct impression that Benjamin couldn't keep anything to himself. I didn't have to worry about him not telling me things. He didn't seem to be able to keep secrets.

"I did," I said. "I deleted it."

"You didn't like it?"

I decided to go with the easiest explanation.

"One of my clients was talking about her experiences using one of the dating apps. I wanted to understand more about how it worked, so I signed up. I only had it a few days."

I didn't tell him that the real reason I had signed up on the dating app was to distract myself from thinking about him. That was one of those things that it seemed best to keep to myself.

"I had it on my phone, too," he said. "I also deleted it."

"Oh? Why did you delete it?"

"I don't care for dating on apps."

"I see." That wasn't the best answer he could have given, but it sounded like the truth.

"Besides," he said. "I've already met the girl I want to date."

My heart skipped a beat. I wanted to think that he was talking about me, but I had no way of knowing that.

"Unfortunately," he said. "She lives on the other side of the country."

"Well," I said. "You're a pilot. Don't pilots have a different perspective about location than most people?"

"We do," I said. "For the most part. But that doesn't make it any easier."

"No. I don't suppose it does."

My heart was sinking now. He was telling me that we lived too far apart to have a relationship. I already knew that, but I didn't want him to actually say it. I was hoping for some other outcome, although in all honesty, I couldn't imagine what that outcome might be.

"We've got the moment, though, right?" he asked.

"Yes," I said, forcing an optimism I didn't feel into my voice. "We have tonight."

Either way, whether we called it the moment or the night, I knew it wasn't going to be enough for me.

What he was implying was us having a casual relationship.

Most people would probably be okay with that.

But I wasn't good at casual. Maybe I was too serious, but casual wasn't something I cared to do.

Chapter Thirty-Six
BENJAMIN

As Peter drove us back toward Grace's townhouse, Grace looked out the window.

I didn't mind the quietness, but I did mind the look on her face.

She seemed quieter than usual. Something was definitely bothering her.

We had to stop in traffic for five minutes while a freight train passed.

"Are you okay?" I asked.

"Just tired, I guess."

"I kept you out past your bedtime. You have early clients?"

"Not really. My first one is at ten o'clock, but I have a lot of rescheduling to do with Jonathan's clients."

"Guess you decided against looking into an assistant."

"Did you hear back from Mrs. Worthington?"

"She's checking into it and will get back to me. I can ask her again. See if she has someone who can get you through this."

"No. Don't do that. I can do it. It just takes a little time. It would take longer to train someone than if I just do it myself."

"Okay."

I liked it a whole lot better when Grace was optimistic. Right now she sounded, I don't know, a little defeated.

I had no doubt that she was tired. She'd worked late, then I'd dragged her out to dinner.

I'd thought that maybe we could stop by Jonathan's room at the hospital, but it had quickly gotten too late. He would be asleep by now.

The train passed by and Peter started moving again.

"I'll have you home soon," I said. "And you can get your beauty rest."

"I don't know about that," she said with a little laugh. "I have a little work to get done tonight."

Maybe I was beginning to understand Tiffany a little bit better.

I was used to being the one who worked all the time. The one who was gone, sometimes for days at the time.

Now, it seemed, things were turned around on me. Grace was the one who worked all the time.

But we were both career people and it was to be expected. We would work through it.

When Peter pulled up in front of her townhouse, she turned to me.

"You don't have to walk me to the door. I'll be okay."

"I can see you to the door."

"It's late," she said. "I can let myself in."

The car came to a stop.

"Are you sure?"

"I'm sure," she said. "I'll talk to you later."

She opened her own door and before I could do anything else, she was out of the car and halfway to her door.

Peter, gentleman that he was, waited until she was inside.

"Shall I wait, Sir?" he asked after she was safely inside.

"No," I said. "Just take me to Jonathan's. It's late. I know you're ready to get home."

"Yes sir."

As we drove away, I saw one of the lights click on inside Grace's townhouse.

Something had changed. I couldn't put my finger on it, but something was different.

Chapter Thirty-Seven

GRACE

I changed into tights and a t-shirt, then sat down at my desk to finish up my charting for the day.

I liked to start off each day caught up from the last. That sometimes meant some late nights that bled over into my reading time.

It was worth it, though, to start each day off fresh.

As long as I was working I wasn't thinking about Benjamin.

At least not much.

Everything had gotten tangled up.

After I had rather accidentally gotten close to him, I belatedly realized that getting close to him wasn't such a good idea.

He was getting ready to return to Pittsburgh.

A long distance relationship that worked for any amount of time was rare. Mostly they just didn't.

What I'd heard Benjamin propose was a casual relationship.

That fit with the reputation of pilots. A girl in every port and all that.

As much as I liked Benjamin, I didn't want to settle for a casual relationship with him.

I couldn't do it. It just wasn't in my nature.

I had rather gotten past the whole thing with him being my client. He had ended up in my office by being Jonathan's friend.

There was no need for me to keep the door open for him to return as a client.

Tapping the edge of my desk, I went with my impulse and pulled up the file I had made with his name on it.

I opened it up, but I didn't have to read it. I remembered everything about Benjamin.

It was time for me to make a decision.

Holding my breath, I clicked the delete button.

The program had a safety feature to prevent accidental deletions.

I had to type the word DELETE to complete the process.

I typed it. And hit enter.

Done.

Without a written record, a session never happened.

So my session with Benjamin had never happened.

He hadn't paid me, so there wouldn't be any record at all.

I had rewritten history.

There was no need for a consultation. No need to tell Jonathan.

It would just be one of those things between me and Benjamin.

If he chose to tell anyone, I would deal with that then.

I was prepared to claim that he and I had simply had a conversation while he waited for Jonathan.

Now all I had to do was delete him from my brain.

That was going to be harder to do.

Unfortunately, there was no place in my brain to type in DELETE and wipe him from my memory.

The best thing I could do was to try to keep myself from thinking about him as much as possible and I certainly didn't need to see him again. Seeing him again would just make things worse. Make it harder to get over him.

After tonight, I doubted he would want to see me again anyway. I'd practically run from the car and hadn't even said goodnight.

A complete one eighty from the night before.

He would figure out that I didn't want to see him anymore.

But. It wasn't true. I wanted to see him very much. More than anything.

It was best for me if I didn't see him anymore.

He was already moving on in his head. Talking about Pittsburgh. A sure sign that he was already moving on.

He rarely came to Houston and that wasn't likely to change.

I couldn't just sit here and wait for him to show up.

Now that I'd made my decision, I expected to feel better. Unfortunately I couldn't say that I did. If anything I felt even more out of sorts.

With my work done, I powered off my computer and went to the sofa to read.

It was best if I didn't think about Benjamin.

Thinking about anything was better than thinking about Benjamin.

I was a psychologist. I should be able to control my thoughts. Right?

Chapter Thirty-Eight
BENJAMIN

The wide deserted halls of the hospitals carried an antiseptic scent. Someone in a room I walked past was listening to a game show.

I passed the nurse's station where three staff members had their eyes focused on computers.

What, I wondered, did people do before computers and cell phones? I couldn't even imagine a world without them. Listening to my parents and grandparents talk about typing on typewriters and long distance phone calls seemed impossible. It was like they had grown up in the dark ages and yet it wasn't all that long ago.

Reaching Jonathan's room, I stopped and knocked on the door.

"Come in," he said.

"Seriously?" I asked, stepping into his room and looking pointedly at his computer.

He had his laptop computer on the little rolling table over his bed and was typing away.

Speaking of computers...

Tiffany sat on the chair next to him, her attention focused on her iPad.

"Yes. He even works in the hospital," she said, but there was no venom in her statement. Just a bit of amusement.

Apparently they had worked out whatever it was that had been bothering them.

All couples, it seemed had things they kept between themselves.

Grace and I had only known each other for days and already we had couples secrets.

"I thought you'd be out of here by now," Jonathan said.

"Yeah, well. I had something to keep me around."

"I'm just gonna go get us some ice water," Tiffany said, making her exit.

Jonathan closed his computer and looked at me.

"Would that something happen to be Grace?"

"It might have been," I said, sitting in the chair Tiffany had vacated.

"Might have been, but isn't now?"

"That's about as good a way to put it as any."

"What happened?"

"I don't know," I said.

One of the nurses came in to check his vitals. He sat quietly while she checked his blood pressure and I did the same.

"Surely you have some idea," Jonathan said after we were alone again.

"I guess I don't have your mind reading ability."

Jonathan shrugged.

"Want me to talk to her?"

"Please don't."

"Suit yourself. But I think it's your loss. Grace is one of a kind."

"I agree."

"Huh."

I smiled to myself.

"It's okay," I said. "She stays busy."

Jonathan scowled at me.

"Do you remember what you told me when I claimed to be too busy to date Tiffany?"

"I probably told you that people find time for the things that are important to them."

"And you were right."

"You and Tiffany found the time for each other."

"We did and I wouldn't change a thing about it. But that's okay. If Grace isn't the one for you then she'll find someone when she's ready."

Everything inside me recoiled at his words.

I didn't want Grace to find someone.

I wanted to be her someone.

I already knew that she was my someone.

What I didn't know was what to do about it.

"You'll think of something," Jonathan said.

I looked sideways at him.

"I know I didn't say that out loud."

"You know you don't have to," Jonathan said. "I'm pretty good at reading minds."

I laughed, but I knew that he was only halfway kidding.

Chapter Thirty-Nine
GRACE

The next two weeks passed by uneventfully.

I stayed busy with clients, including several new clients. It was interesting that two of them had been Zoom clients. I could see that psychologists would be doing more and more sessions in that format.

Jonathan returned to his office walking on a pair of crutches and everything seemed to be somewhat back to normal.

I was sitting at my desk, already finished with charting, reading the latest study on dreams in one of my psychology journals, when my phone rang.

"Dr. Miller," I answered, not recognizing the number.

"Hello Dr. Miller. This is Dr. Worthington. Savannah Worthington. I hope I haven't caught you at a bad time."

"No," I said, straightening in my chair as though she could see me. "Not at all. I'm between clients."

"Good," she said. "I just wanted to let you know that I haven't forgotten about you."

"I'm sorry?"

"Benjamin asked me to find you someone. A receptionist."

"Oh. Right. I didn't want him to bother you."

"It's not a bother. We're family. I'm happy to help. He called me this morning, in fact, to follow up."

There was a moment's pause as I tried to figure out how to respond.

"I'm sure that Jonathan will be pleased to have some help. He probably hasn't even recognized the need, knowing him."

"That's a good point," I said. "We've actually gotten rather busy and scheduling is a big part of that, as you know."

Mrs. Worthington laughed. "I'm more than familiar. But I have someone who worked for me in the past. She stopped working to have a family, but now she's ready to come back to work."

I almost told her that I needed to check with Jonathan first. Then I remembered what Benjamin had pointed out. It was my business as much as it was Jonathan's.

If I was unsure, I could start with someone on a temporary basis.

"If you like, I can send you her information."

"That's very kind of you," I said.

"Okay…" she said. "You should have it."

My phone chimed with a message.

"Got it."

"Good. How are you doing Grace?"

"I'm okay," I said, surprised at the question.

"Is there anything else I can do to help? I know things have been busy with Jonathan being out."

"I think we're okay," I said.

"Well. If there is ever anything I can do to help you, this is my personal cell phone number. Call me anytime."

I thanked her and we disconnected the line.

Perplexed, I saved the contact she sent me. I'd give the receptionist a call later in the afternoon. That would give me time to think about what I needed to do.

Benjamin had come through for me. He hadn't forgotten.

He'd contacted Dr. Worthington initially, then he'd taken the time to follow up.

It was unexpected and caused me to have butterflies in my stomach.

I'd tried not to think about Benjamin.

I couldn't say that I was doing very well in that area, but I was giving it my best effort. As a result, I was most definitely getting a lot of work done.

Work, I'd found, was the best distraction against thinking about a handsome, charming pilot from Pittsburgh.

Now Dr. Worthington had called and given me a setback.

I'd had to toss the roses Benjamin had sent me, but I'd filled the vase with daffodils I'd found at my favorite florist shop just that morning.

He had made an indelible impression on my heart.

I might not like it, but I would go on without him.

The fates had not been in our favor.

I didn't regret it though. I didn't regret a single minute of the time I'd spent with him.

If anything, the experience gave me a new perspective that helped me in working with my clients, most of whom were dealing with relationship problems.

I now understood how someone could fall in love at first sight. That and I had a better understanding of what it felt like to have my heart ripped out.

Chapter Forty
BENJAMIN

Business at the Pittsburgh office of Skye Travels was booming.

Maybe it was the time of year. Prime travel time for businesses as always, but also for family vacations. People wanted to get in those last trips before school started.

About fifty percent of my clients over the past couple of weeks had been those families.

The biggest difference was the noise level. Families were noisy. And then there was the luggage. Families brought a whole lot more luggage than the businesspeople I typically flew.

And I couldn't forget the pets. Several of those families brought along their dogs. One even brought a couple of cats.

I didn't normally pay much attention to the families.

Just passengers like any others in my mind. But today I watched them.

I watched as the husband helped his children, then his wife

buckle into her seat. He took her hand and gave her a quick kiss. She was a nervous flyer, I decided.

I envied them. Getting to travel together as a family. I was flying them to Mackinac Island where they would stay for two weeks.

Spending two weeks on Mackinac Island with your wife was enviable material.

I would settle for having Grace sitting next to me in the copilot's seat.

It seemed like a small thing to ask, but it would never happen. She had her psychology practice firmly established in Houston.

I had my work with Skye Travels. In Pittsburgh.

I understood about having an established career.

And yet both my two brothers and my two sisters had married people who also had careers and they had worked it all out so that they were together and happy.

After harnessing myself into my own pilot's seat, I checked my phone. No messages.

Grace's number was in my favorites. I hovered over it. I could call her, but what would I say?

Hi. How are you? I'm on my way to Mackinac Island. Flying a nice family up for a vacation.

I set my phone aside and went through the preflight checklist. Again.

I wanted more from her than just casual conversations now and then. I couldn't much see the point in calling her when I wanted to see her.

Long distance relationships didn't work.

I'd seen that disaster happen more times than I cared to think about.

The only way a pilot could have a real relationship was to be based out of the same city as his girl. Pilots were gone a lot to begin with. Not living in the same city pretty much meant rarely seeing each other.

With the control tower chatter in the background, I taxied out onto the runway.

My heart skipped a beat as a my phone chimed with a text message.

My first thought was that it was Grace.

But it was Uncle Noah.

> **UNCLE NOAH**
> I'm going to be in Pittsburgh tomorrow. Are you available to meet?
>
> Of course.

Uncle Noah was essentially my boss. My uncle, but also my boss.

His message sounded more like a summons from a boss than a message from an uncle.

It was good timing. I had no flights tomorrow.

As I took the airplane into the air, it occurred to me that he probably knew that. Of course he knew that. Uncle Noah didn't get where he was by leaving things to chance.

The airplane swayed as we reached ground effect. I couldn't imagine what Uncle Noah might want with me.

I hadn't met with him on a business matter since the day he

had interviewed me. It hadn't been a traditional interview in any way. We'd gone up in his Phenom with me in the pilot's seat.

It had just been a casual, no stress flight, but apparently I had passed whatever test he had been giving me.

Since then I had only seen him mostly at family gatherings.

He was a busy man, but he somehow made time for family. When I grew up, I wanted to be like Uncle Noah.

Successful and family oriented somehow all at the same time.

I guess I needed that family first. As far as career success went, I was doing what I wanted to do. I didn't have any desire to be a business owner. I had enough money between my family and my work.

I just needed the family. Starting with the girl.

When I saw myself with a family, I pictured myself with Grace.

She was the one.

I had met her by accident, but falling in love with her was no accident.

Falling in love with her had been fate.

Unfortunately, the circumstances keeping us apart were insurmountable.

I turned off the seat belt light and settled in for the flight to Mackinac Island. I would be dropping the family off, then flying right back out.

This trip was no vacation for me.

It wouldn't be a vacation anyway without Grace.

Chapter Forty-One
GRACE

I finished up with another one of my Zoom sessions—my last session for the day—and swiveled around to look out the window.

Because Jonathan didn't like doing virtual sessions, I took them all. I didn't mind. I could still see their body language and I appreciated the convenience of not having to navigate Houston traffic.

Like right now. Cars were backed up with rush hour traffic. Three o'clock on a Friday afternoon was already pretty bad.

In another life, I could imagine myself having a chauffeur like Peter to drive me around while I did client notes in the backseat.

A girl could dream, after all.

I swiveled back around, took a deep swallow of water, then opened up the charting program.

There was no reason to leave the office right now. I'd just be sitting in traffic and since I didn't have anyone to drive me, it would be time lost. Time I could spend filling out paperwork.

With city ambiance behind me—a firetruck and someone's loud music to name a couple of the most notable sounds—I caught up on charting and checked the schedule. Tomorrow would be our new receptionist's first day. Her name was Bonnie Gray and she had a pleasant demeanor that was going to work well with us. Dr. Worthington had given me a good recommendation.

The only downside was that she was going to be working remotely. Giving her space on the floor would mean renting another office and we weren't ready to do that. I didn't know how that was going to go, but I was willing to keep an open mind about it.

With my charting and scheduling finished, I logged out of my computer, stood up to stretch, then grabbed my purse out of the bottom drawer. A glance out the window told me that the traffic was about as manageable as it was going to get.

Thinking about stopping by for a some take out on the way home, I opened my door and froze.

Benjamin stood leaning against the wall across the hall from my office.

"Hi," he said, pushing off the wall and walking toward me.

"Hi." Since I couldn't get my feet to move, I stood where I was.

Standing in front of me, he ran a hand along a strand of hair that had fallen out of my clip. A very intimate gesture from someone I hadn't seen or heard from for almost three weeks.

"Are you here to see Jonathan?" I asked.

"I'm here to see you," he said.

"Do you... want to come in?" Maybe I had been wrong. Maybe he did want to see me for a session.

"I was thinking more like I'd take you to dinner."

"So… this is a social call?"

He narrowed his eyes at me.

"As opposed to what?"

"I don't know," I said with a little shrug. "I thought maybe you wanted to talk about something."

"I do want to talk to you about something, but not as a client."

"Okay," I said, locking the door behind me, my hands shaking a little.

"I hear your new receptionist starts tomorrow."

"How do you know that?"

"I had dinner with Uncle Noah and Aunt Savannah last night."

"Right." I had forgotten momentarily that he was the nephew of a tycoon.

"You were a big topic of conversation." He pressed the elevator button.

"Me?" I asked, genuinely surprised.

"Yes. You."

"What did I do?" I said it lightly, but I was actually concerned. His aunt—Dr. Savannah Worthington—might have heard about our session. I could be in trouble.

"Feeling guilty about something?" he asked with a little smile.

"No," I said. "I'm not feeling guilty."

"Good."

We stepped on the elevator and rode down in silence.

"You want me to meet you somewhere?" I asked. I was giving

him a hard time. Maybe I was a little wary of him. Not staying in touch and then just showing up like this.

"Not what I had in mind," he said. "Since tomorrow is Saturday, we can get your car later."

Did he know I didn't work tomorrow or was he just making assumptions?

Curious nonetheless, I followed him out the front door to a sleek black Maserati.

He opened the door, but I didn't get in right away.

"This is your car."

"You remembered."

"Psychologists don't forget anything," I said, sliding into the passenger seat.

"Don't I know it?" He closed my door and headed around to the driver's seat.

"Seriously," I said as he pulled out onto the main road. "How is your car here? Do you have a transport plane now?"

"Something like that."

I looked at him sideways, but decided to let it go. For now at least.

"Where are you taking me?" I asked.

"Someplace that has white table cloths and candles on the tables."

"Sounds formal."

"You don't have anything against formal, do you?"

"I like formal."

"Good."

"But I'm not dressed for formal."

"It's okay. Aunt Savannah sent something for you."

"What?"

He gestured over his shoulder. I followed his gaze. There was a clothes bag laying across the back seat.

"What's that?"

"It's a formal dress. You can change… when we get there."

"You're full of surprises tonight."

He flashed a grin before merging onto the freeway heading north.

I didn't know of any nice restaurants north of town.

Thinking maybe he knew something I didn't, I relaxed against the butter soft leather seat and occupied my mind with wondering just how he came to be here, with his car no less.

"Did you drive from Pittsburgh?" I asked.

"God. No. I like driving in city traffic. Not across the country."

"Huh."

He smiled.

"You have a place in mind?" I asked. I'd have to come back to the whole car thing.

"I do. In fact, we have reservations."

It was a little early for dinner, but I decided to keep that comment to myself.

When he exited off the freeway onto the airport road, I realized where we were going.

"We're going to the airport?" I asked.

"You figured it out."

"But why?"

"We have reservations."

"At the airport."

"If I tell you, it won't be a surprise."

"Maybe I don't like surprises," I said.

"Tell me it's not so," he said with a look of shock that I hoped was contrived.

"Maybe sometimes surprises are okay," I said.

"That's a relief. I thought we were going to need couples therapy there for a minute."

"Couples therapy. Sometimes you're very confusing."

Very was putting it mildly. I hadn't seen or heard from him for three weeks and now he was here and he was talking about us going to couples therapy.

He pulled into the airport parking lot and came around to open my door and grab the dress off the back seat.

"This is highly unusual," I said.

He tossed the dress bag over his shoulder and took my hand with the other.

"Who wants to go through life doing the usual?"

I didn't answer, because, truly he had a good point.

We walked straight out onto the tarmac to a private jet with Skye Travels painted along the fuselage.

"Wait," I said, stopping. "We're going flying?"

"You don't like flying?"

"I don't know. I mean yes. But I don't know. I've never flown on a private jet."

"Then you are in for a pleasant experience."

After he pressed a button to lower the steps, we climbed inside.

The airplane was small. Two rows of leather seats.

"This way," he said, dropping the dress bag over one of the seats.

I followed him to the front of the airplane.

"This is your seat," he said. "And this is mine."

"Okay." I sat down in what I figured was the copilot's seat and waited while he sat in the pilot's seat.

"Where are we headed?" I asked.

"Part of the surprise."

He reached over and secured my harness. Handed me a headset.

"You can wear this if you want to."

I held it as he slid his own headset over his head.

"You don't have to wear it," he said. "It just makes talking easier."

I slid the headset on over my head and situated it.

"Why wouldn't I wear it?" I asked into the microphone.

His answer came through the headset loud and clear in my ears.

"A lot of girls think it messes up their hair."

"Is that so?" I asked, wondering how many girls he had taken flying.

"Approach runway three," the air traffic controller said through our headsets, distracting me from going down that line of thinking.

Besides, I liked watching Benjamin. He handled the plane with the confidence that went with being a pilot.

He was handsome in his pilot's uniform, especially the captain's cap.

I reminded myself, a little belatedly perhaps, not to get too close to him. I didn't even know why he was here all of a sudden.

I sighed.

"What's that about?"

"What?"

"You sighed."

I smiled with a little shrug.

How could I explain how happy I was to see him and at the same time I was afraid to be happy about seeing him.

Just being here with him like this was giving me butterflies in my stomach.

"Cleared for takeoff."

"You ready?" Benjamin asked, looking over at me.

I nodded.

He squeezed my hand, then took the plane into the air.

It swayed as we left the ground and then just like that we were in the air heading toward the clouds.

I settled back in my seat.

This was going to be fun.

I had no reason not to enjoy the evening.

I was in control of my thoughts. Right?

Chapter Forty-Two
BENJAMIN

It was a perfect evening for a flight. The sky was blue with cumulus clouds scattered here and there.

The sun would be setting to our left before long.

With Grace sitting in the copilot's seat next to me, I was content.

It had taken some work to make this evening happen, but it was all worth it.

I had things to tell her.

Things I hoped she wanted to hear.

I didn't want to consider the possibility that she might not want to hear what I had to say.

We reached ten thousand feet and I set the airplane on autopilot. Ten thousand feet was my favorite altitude. High enough, but not too high to see the world below us. Rivers and roads still looked like rivers and roads.

I wanted to share everything with her. Especially flying. Flying was who I was. I wanted her to be part of my life and flying was a good place to start.

She sat quietly, taking in everything from everything I did to the view below.

We flew in companionable silence until the airplane started its descent.

"Are you taking me to Canada?" she asked.

"Very close," I said. "You're very close."

As we approached Mackinac Island, I took the scenic route over the island, flying so that she could see the Grand Hotel from her window.

"Wait," she said, glancing back at me for a split second. "Where are we?"

"Mackinac Island."

"This looks familiar," she said, her brow creased.

We left the hotel's air space and neared the airport.

"The Grand Hotel," I said.

I saw the moment she put it together.

"Somewhere in Time. The Grand Hotel."

"You know the movie?"

"It was only the most romantic movie ever made."

"It was filmed here."

"No it wasn't," she said, without conviction, looking out her window again.

"It was."

"I didn't know it was a real place."

I knew by the awe in her voice that I had made the right choice in bringing her here.

"It is. Only there are no cars allowed. The only way to get here is by boat or by plane."

"It's beautiful," she said as we went in for a landing.

"It's one of my favorite places," I said.

"We're having dinner here?"

"At the Grand Hotel."

As I taxied along the runway, she looked around at the maple trees.

"If there are no cars allowed, how do we get to the hotel?"

"We take a taxi," I said.

"Part of the surprise?" she asked.

"Do you like it so far?" I asked.

"Are you kidding? I love it."

"Then yes. It's part of the surprise. We're a few minutes early. By the time I secure the airplane, our taxi should be here."

So far. So good. I wanted the evening to be perfect.

Chapter Forty-Three
GRACE

The taxi turned out to be a horse and buggy with a formally dressed driver.

A different type of chauffeur than Peter, but still a chauffeur.

The sun was starting its descent over the horizon by the time we were settled into the buggy and the sun took the warmth of the day with it.

The buggy came with a warm wool blanket that Benjamin spread over our laps.

After leaving the airport, the driver took us along a wide paved road lined with a thousand maple trees that could easily be a road for cars if cars were allowed.

"It's so beautiful here," I said.

"You should see it in the fall when the leaves turn red."

"I'll add it to my list," I said.

"Your bucket list?"

"No. I don't have one of those."

The horse's clip clop blended with the sound of a ferry's horn in the distance.

"I'm curious now," Benjamin said. "What list?"

"Just things I want to do."

"How is that different from a bucket list?"

"It's hard to explain."

He took my hand and squeezed.

"Give it a go."

"Okay." I took a deep breath. How did I explain it? "There's probably not a whole lot of difference. A bucket list is a list of things a person wants to do in their lifetime, right?"

"That's my understanding."

"Well. If there's something I want to do, I put it on the list of things I want to do by the end of the year."

"Makes sense," he said.

"How so?"

"You don't like to put things off until the last minute."

"That's right," I said, looking into his clear blue eyes.

"but what if you don't do it by the end of the year?"

"Then I reassess and if I still want to do it, it goes on next year's list."

Benjamin laughed.

"My dear," he said. "I think you have a bucket list and you don't know it."

"I like to call my list goals and aspirations."

"You'll get no argument from me. I have a tendency to make things happen, too."

"Is that so?" I looked at him sideways.

"Why do you think we're here?"

"Why are we here?" I asked before I could change my mind.

I wanted to know and at the same time I feared the answer.

If he just wanted company for the evening, then I didn't really want to know.

I didn't know what it was I wanted from him, but I knew that it would never be enough.

But right now in one of the most romantic places I'd ever been, was not the time to think about that.

I'd think about that later.

Right now all I needed to do was to think about enjoying the evening.

The handsome man I had fallen head over heels for had flown me to the romantic Mackinac Island that I didn't even know existed until now on a private jet and we were going to have dinner at the Grand Hotel.

Any girl in her right mind would love a fairy tale evening like this one.

Chapter Forty-Four
BENJAMIN

The driver of the buggy stopped in front of the Grand Hotel.

I had to tamp down the unexpected feelings of nervousness I was feeling.

I'd pulled this evening together and everything that went with it. And now that it was here, I hoped that I was doing the right thing.

Grace was star-struck by the Grand Hotel. I had no doubts about that part.

The rest of it remained to be seen.

I climbed out of the buggy, then reached up and, taking Grace by the waist, set her on the ground next to me.

I grabbed the dress bag and slung it over my shoulder.

"It's black tie?" Grace asked as another couple, wearing formal dress clothes walked past us.

"Close enough."

"When do I need to change clothes?"

"How about now?" I said, opening the door to the Grand Hotel.

We found a dressing room where she could change. Apparently we weren't the only ones who had to make last minute wardrobe changes.

Before I left her, I unzipped the bag and pulled out my own tuxedo jacket.

"You aren't the only one who has to change," I said.

"Good to know. Want to put your other one in here?"

"Sure." I shrugged out of my jacket and hung it back in the bag. "See you in a few minutes."

While she changed clothes, I wandered out onto the porch—the longest porch in the world, but I didn't go far.

White egrets dipped low over the water, calling out for each other as a ferry, packed with tourists, left the island headed for the main land.

Like Grace, I had more of a right now or soon list than a bucket list. And my right now list now included bringing Grace back to the island when the leaves started changing. Maybe even for the *Somewhere in Time* festival if she wanted to go to that.

But right now, we were going to have dinner in one of the most romantic places in the country.

I wandered back to the dressing room where I had left her.

Grace was a good sport. I had to give her that. She let me fly her up here. Changed into the dress I had brought her. Maybe. I hadn't seen it yet, but Aunt Savannah had insisted that it would be appropriate and somehow she seemed convinced that it would fit Grace.

We were about to find out. Even if the dress didn't fit or Grace didn't like it, her work clothes would be okay for dinner in the Grand Hotel.

If not, then there was a dress shop down the hall where we could buy her a dress.

The dressing room door opened and Grace stepped out.

I now had the answer to my question.

Chapter Forty-Five
GRACE

I HAD to admit that I was dubious about wearing a dress sight unseen that belonged to someone else.

When I unzipped the bag, however, I found that the dress still had the tags on it. I looked at the price tag twice to make sure I was seeing it right.

The dress cost more than I made in a month. A good month.

So Dr. Savannah Worthington had sent Benjamin off with a new dress for me to wear.

I didn't understand that, but the dress was far too beautiful for me to complain about.

It was a long dress in a sparkly silver color. Simple with long sleeves.

When I put it on, it fit perfectly and looked stunning. I could not have done better if I'd had the dress custom made for myself.

Since I wasn't sure what to do with the price tag, I left it alone.

I put my own shoes back on. For once wearing heels to work made sense.

After putting my work clothes in the dress bag along with Benjamin's jacket, I zipped it all back up.

It was a little odd having our clothes in there together. Odd in a good way. Intimate almost.

I opened the door and found Benjamin waiting for me.

He took the garment bag from me.

"Do you like the dress?" he asked.

"What's not to like? It's a perfect fit." I made a twirl.

"Uh oh."

"What?" Alarm swirled through me. Had I missed a zipper? Put it on backwards?

"We have to get this tag off."

He reached over and gave the tag a pull.

"I didn't know if Dr. Worthington wanted it back."

"It's yours now," he said. "Consider it a gift."

"It's too much," I said, watching him stuff the tag into his pocket.

"Let's take a walk on the longest porch in the world," he said, ignoring my concern.

He took my hand and led me out onto the porch. The long porch stood several feet high with a paved road running along below it.

There were pots of flowers everywhere. Bright red geraniums. There must be hundreds of them. And hundreds of white rocking chairs lined down the porch. And American flags hanging off the side of the porch every few feet. Music from someone playing a cello drifted from the hotel lobby.

Everything was done on a grand scale.

We stopped and looked out toward Lake Huron. It looked like an ocean with colorful gardens between here and there.

"You're wondering why I brought you here," Benjamin said, propping an arm on the railing and facing me.

"A little. Yes." I looked into his blue eyes. "Maybe a lot."

He seemed a little nervous, shifting from one foot to the other. He glanced out over the lake. A horse and buggy with a couple nestled together clip clopped along below us.

He returned his gaze to mine and looked questioningly into my eyes.

"I flew a family here last week and I thought of you."

"I see."

"It made me think about a lot of things."

"What kind of things?"

"I don't want to wake up every morning and see myself in the bathroom mirror."

"Who do you want to see?" I asked with a little laugh.

He took my hand and pressed his forehead against mine.

"You," he said. "I want to wake up and see you."

My heart turned upside down sending my thoughts into a tailspin.

"Me?"

"Sure. Why not you?"

"Well..." Why not me indeed? "I think maybe because you live in Pittsburgh and I lived in Houston."

"And yet here we are." He pulled me against him into a tight hug.

After a second, I relaxed against him, resting my head against his chest. His chin fit just right on the top of my head.

A ferry's mournful whistle blew three times along with the clip clop of another horse and buggy passing by on the road below.

I don't know how long we stood there, but when I opened my eyes, the full moon reflected off the water.

"So," he said, pulling me toward one of the benches where we sat side by side.

"So?"

"So… what if I didn't live in Pittsburgh?"

"Where would you live?"

"What if I lived in Houston?"

I closed my eyes for a brief minute. Reminded myself that he was not a client.

"Then, I guess, we would be having a different conversation."

"Okay," he said with an amused expression. "Let's have a different conversation."

"Okay." I nodded. "How would this conversation go?"

I didn't really like this game. I had a feeling this game was going to play on my emotions.

He rubbed his chin and seemed to consider.

"You know I'll be gone a lot, right? Flying and all."

"I know you're a pilot. Yes."

"You'd be okay with that?"

"I'd have to be, wouldn't I?"

"I would have weekends off most of the time."

A pleasant bell rang, interrupting our conversation.

"What's that for?" I asked.

"It's the dinner bell. We're supposed to go inside."

Thank goodness for small favors.

I liked talking to Benjamin. I liked talking to him a lot. But I did not like playing this game with him.

Chapter Forty-Six
BENJAMIN

I sat next to Grace at a corner table with a white table cloth, a candle, and a red geranium in a vase in the middle of the table.

Outside, the moonlight glowed over Lake Huron.

Inside the Grand Hotel restaurant, the steady hum of conversation blended with the soft strains of a young lady playing the cello.

We had wine in our glasses, but I didn't touch mine. Since I had to fly back tonight, I had to consider the whole bottle to throttle rule.

Grace looked troubled.

I hadn't meant to upset her by talking about me living in Houston. She didn't seem too happy about it, all in all.

Maybe I would need to come back to it.

"Tell me how things are going at work. How is your new assistant working out?"

"She starts work tomorrow," Grace said. "She's going to be working remotely though."

"That's how things are done now, right?"

"Seems to be. I'm actually seeing a lot of clients over the Internet."

"For counseling? How is that working?"

"It's working better than I expected. Quite well actually."

"Hmm." I leaned back and considered this. If she was seeing clients remotely, then maybe she could travel some with me after all.

This might work out better than I thought.

"You like seeing clients remotely?"

"I do actually kind of like it. I'd probably like it better if I didn't have to go in to the office."

I grinned.

"What's funny?" she asked.

"Nothing is funny. Everything is perfect."

The server came and took our order.

"Save room for the dessert," the server said before he walked off. "You don't want to miss the Grand Pecan Balls."

"What's a grand pecan ball?" Grace asked.

"It's their signature dessert."

"Have you had it then?"

"Yes. He's right. It's something we don't want to miss out on."

She swirled the wine in her glass. Took a little sip.

"This is…" she glanced around before locking her gaze on mine. "so unexpected."

"I hope you like it."

"I'm not sure how someone could come here and not like it."

"It could happen."

"Is your family well?" she asked, smoothly and obviously changing the subject.

"Insane as ever," I said.

"But you love them very much."

"Yes. I do."

"So in your hypothetical world, you would miss your family."

"We have enough pilots in the family that I'm sure we'd see each other often enough."

"Good point." She sat back in her chair and looked at me sideways as though she was trying to figure something out.

She referred to my world as hypothetical. It occurred to me that she didn't know that I wasn't referring to a hypothetical world.

I had been rather vague.

Perhaps it was time to make myself clear.

Chapter Forty-Seven
GRACE

The Grand Pecan Balls lived up to their reputation and perhaps more.

I didn't eat a lot of desserts, but the pecan balls with caramel sauce were decadently good.

I glanced at my watch. Calculated the flight time back.

We were going to be out late, but since it was Saturday night, I didn't have to be at work tomorrow.

It had been… a long time since I'd had a date. Tonight I was coming back into dating with a blast.

"Have you talked to Jonathan?" I asked.

"No," Benjamin said. "Not lately."

"It's the whole guy thing," I said. "Where you can go for years without talking, then just pick up like no time has passed at all."

"I guess it is."

"Something's bothering you?"

"Well, Doctor," he said, leaning forward on his elbows. "I'd like to go back to that conversation we were having earlier."

"Do we have to?" I asked.

"Is the idea of me living nearby so distasteful then?"

"Quite the opposite," I said. "I feel like you're toying with my emotions."

"Okay," he said, taking my hands across the table. "Let me start over."

"Sure."

"I'll start at the beginning. Noah needs someone in Houston. A pilot. And he asked me if I'd relocate. To Houston."

"Wait. So it's not a hypothetical."

"No. That's why my car is in Houston."

Of course. It all made sense now. He had his car in Houston because he was living there now.

"So you're living in Houston now?"

"I have everything set up. But… if you tell me to, I can unravel everything and go back to Pittsburgh. It all hinges on you."

"I don't understand why it hinges on me. Houston is a big city."

"And don't you think I'd be looking at you at every turn. Every time I visited Jonathan."

I would certainly be looking for him. In fact, even now I often looked up toward my door, hoping to see him standing there.

"I get that."

"So what do you think? Can I stay in Houston?"

I smiled, biting my lower lip.

"You can stay."

"Good. Now. Can we talk some more about that? Because I have some ideas."

"What kind of ideas?"

"I'm thinking that you can move your clients, some of them at least, to online and you can travel with me."

The young lady playing the cello stopped to take a break and the conversations in the restaurant dropped a level to accommodate.

"I think you missed a few steps in there," I said, pulling my hands away and taking another sip of my wine.

"I probably did," I said. "But sometimes a guy has to just cut to the chase."

"So you're saying you're moving to Houston, leaving your family in Pittsburgh, and you want me to travel with you."

"Yes. How does that sound?"

"It sounds interesting."

"I'm not talking about a hypothetical," he said.

"I know." I smiled a little. "But can you be a little more specific?"

"I can, but…" He stopped talking and looked at me with an odd expression on his face.

"But…?"

"Yes." He held up a finger. "Give me just a minute." He stood up, unzipped the dress bag tossed across one of the chairs at our table, and dug into the pocket of his jacket.

"I can be very specific," he said, sitting back down, holding something in his hand.

"What do you have there?" I asked. "You're worrying me a little bit."

"You don't ever have to be worried. Not ever. Not with me."

I knew he was right. I never had to worry with him.

As for the implications of that, I couldn't say.

Chapter Forty-Eight
BENJAMIN

Early today when I'd been doing a preflight check of the airplane, I had come across a loose O-ring. I'd brought it to the attention of one of the mechanics and he'd replaced it right away. I had absently dropped the loose O-ring into my jacket pocket. It was a small red rubber circle.

Grace, sitting across from me, looking beautifully perplexed or maybe perplexingly beautiful, had no idea just what an O-ring could mean to a guy.

Grace had agreed that she would like for me to live in Houston. That was a good first step.

She hadn't, however, committed to anything more.

The O-ring was the missing link. Or at least it would serve as the missing link for right now.

And still I waited. I waited until the server had cleared off the table.

And I waited until the cello player was back at work, spilling romantic music through the room.

Then I slid off my seat onto one knee, right in front of her.

"Grace," I said.

She was looking at me with wide, disbelieving eyes.

"I hadn't planned on doing this tonight. I wanted to wait. But now I know that I don't need to wait. I'm not really prepared, so you'll have to forgive me."

I held up the O-ring.

She looked at it the way any girl would look at an O-ring.

"What's that?"

"This is a temporary token to be replaced by a more fitting token at the first possible moment."

She was frowning at me now and I expected no less.

"Grace. Dr. Grace Miller. Will you marry me?"

"I..." She just looked at me, then down at the O-ring, and back again. "What?"

"Will you spend the rest of your life with me? I want you to be my wife."

"But..."

I held up the O-ring. "Temporary."

"You want to marry me?" she asked. "But you hardly know me."

"I've known since the moment I first saw you that you were the one."

"I don't know what to say."

"Yes?"

I slid the O-ring on her finger.

"It's a little big," I said. "We'll have to get it resized."

She looked at me with such horror that I laughed.

"I'm kidding. Tomorrow. Tomorrow we'll go to Tiffany's and trade it in."

"No," she said, pulling her hand back. My heart took a nose dive.

I nodded and leaned back.

This wasn't what she wanted. It was okay. But I wasn't giving up.

"I won't trade it in," she said.

"Does that mean you'll marry me?"

With tears in her eyes, she nodded.

"Yes. I'll marry you." The words seemed to stick in her throat.

Everyone in the restaurant—I had forgotten that there was anyone else around—clapped.

"We had an audience," I said, sitting back on my chair.

"I think they like us," she said.

"I think you're right." I stood up and pulled her to her feet. "Can we seal it with a kiss?"

She nodded again and I pressed my lips against hers.

The rest of the world vanished.

Chapter Forty-Nine

GRACE

Monday morning I sat at my desk, my chair turned to face the traffic below. I'd gotten to work early, before the traffic got bad.

The sun was up now, the early morning light of dawn reflecting off the glass walls of the skyscraper across the road.

I held up my left hand and admired the ring on my finger.

The Tiffany diamond solitaire sparkled on my left hand. Benjamin had been true to his word.

I wore the red O-ring on my index finger. Oddly enough, the O-ring meant as much to me as the expensive diamond.

Benjamin had given the O-ring to me spontaneously in the heat of the moment, proposing to me in the Grand Hotel main restaurant in front of everyone.

As I replayed the memory again, as I had, over and over, it warmed my heart.

I had thought that Benjamin had been talking hypothetically

to me about moving to Houston. But he had arranged to move here.

And he wanted me to travel with him.

He wanted to marry me.

The whole thing still felt surreal.

I was by far the luckiest girl on the planet.

I should be getting ready for my first client, but I wanted to take just another minute to bask in the memory of our evening on Mackinac Island.

A knock at the door jarred me out of my thoughts.

I swiveled around to find Jonathan, on crutches, making his way toward my desk.

"Am I interrupting?" he asked.

"Of course not," I said, putting my hands in my lap. "I was just thinking."

"We don't take the time to do enough of that, do we?"

He carefully lowered himself into one of the two chairs across from my desk.

"Do you want to sit on the sofa?" I asked. "They tell me it's more comfortable."

"No. I won't be long."

"Okay," I said, waiting for him to tell me why he was here.

Jonathan rarely visited my office. We were both busy and we communicated primarily by text if it was quick or email if it was something longer.

Even though he claimed he wouldn't be long, he laid down his crutches, leaned back in his chair, and seemed to make himself comfortable.

"There's something I haven't told you."

"Oh?" I leaned forward, curious now.

Jonathan rarely shared personal information with me.

"It's about Tiffany."

"Is she okay? You reconciled, right?"

"She's good. We're good. This is about how the two of us met."

"You met at an art showing, right?"

"We did. That is true. But there's more to the story."

"I see." I ran a finger over the diamond on my left hand. "And you feel the need to share this with me now because...?"

"I'm not sure," he said.

I nodded. He knew exactly why he wanted to tell me this now. Jonathan never did anything on accident... except fall down the stairs. He was the most intentional person I knew.

"We initially met at an art gallery. But then she showed up at my office."

"That doesn't sound unusual."

"As a client."

"Wait." I pressed my hands together and almost put them on the desk, but I wasn't ready to tell him about Benjamin. "She was your client?"

"Sort of. Yes. We had one session."

"So she came in for a session, but you already knew her. You recognized her?"

"How could I not? I fell in love with her at first sight."

I smiled. I knew that Jonathan was crazy about Tiffany and always had been.

"What did you do?"

"I talked to her. But I knew I couldn't work with her."

"But technically... you had one session with her."

"I don't know if I'd even really call it a session."

"Did you refer her?"

"I offered. But she didn't really need counseling. I can't tell you what it was, but it was temporary."

"You didn't worry about the overlap between her being a client and a... girlfriend?"

"There was nothing to worry about."

"I still don't understand why you're telling me this," I said. And yet I had alarm bells going off in my head. He knew something about me and Benjamin.

"I guess I just wanted to let you know that it's okay for you to date Benjamin."

"Okay."

"There are some things that defy logic. If you find one of those things, I think you should go with it."

"Thank you for saying so," I said.

"Sure thing." He picked up his crutches and I thought he was going to leave, but he stopped and looked at me.

"I'm not sure how exactly you met Benjamin, but I wanted to let you know that however it came about, I think the two of you make a good couple."

It would have been a good time for me to hold up my hand. To show him that he was right about whatever it was he sensed between me and Benjamin.

But I didn't. Instead, I watched as Jonathan, the closest thing to a mind reader as I had ever met, cross the room on his crutches. Even with the crutches, he looked confident as he should.

He stopped at the door and turned around.

"Grace," he said. "Don't let a good thing pass you by. Some things are worth the risk."

He turned and continued making his way down the hall.

"I won't," I said to myself, swiveling around again and swirling the O-ring that Benjamin had put on my finger.

Jonathan had just revealed to me that he had been in a similar situation as I had been with Benjamin and he had given me permission to date Benjamin.

It wasn't that I needed his permission.

But I was certainly more than relieved to have it.

Needing to move around, I walked down the hallway to the restroom and looked into the mirror.

I was glowing in that way of the newly engaged. If anyone could see it, it would be Jonathan.

Maybe he didn't actually know yet about my engagement to Benjamin, but he saw it coming. He had to.

He'd probably seen it coming before I had.

Chapter Fifty
BENJAMIN

I WAITED for Grace outside her office to take her to lunch.

We didn't have a date and I didn't even know her schedule. But I was content to wait.

I didn't have any flights today and I had just finished up my orientation for the Houston office. It was mostly a formality since I was from the Pittsburgh office and everything pretty much ran the same way in both offices.

Different faces. Same paperwork.

I looked away as her client left. I didn't need to intrude on her client's privacy.

But I did need to intrude on her.

She was just going to have to get used to me being around. If I wasn't flying, I had every intention of being with her.

I had rented a furnished condo, but I didn't plan to be in it much.

We could live in her townhouse if she wanted to or we could look for a place of our own.

I went to her door and leaned against the door casing.

She immediately looked up and I saw the welcome that spread across her face.

"Hi," I said.

"Hi."

Without waiting for an invitation, I walked across to her desk and held out the single red rose I held behind my back.

She smiled as she took it from me.

She wore the Tiffany's diamond on her finger along with the red O-ring I had given her at the Grand Hotel.

I found it absolutely charming that she wore the O-ring. I hadn't intended for her to actually wear it, but she refused to give it up.

"Want to go to lunch?" I asked.

Her answer was to pull her purse out of the bottom draw of her desk where she kept it.

"You know," she said as she came around the desk. "You have be careful. I could get used to this."

"I have every intention of you getting used to it."

She slid the rose into a vase of daffodils on her desk.

"That's an interesting look," I said.

"I'll fix it later." She shrugged. "The daffodils need to be tossed anyway."

"If I'd know that, I would have brought more than one rose."

"But one is perfect," she said.

We walked companionably to the elevator and waited for it to open up.

"Did you happen to say something to Jonathan?" she asked after we were inside the elevator.

"I haven't spoken to him."

"Huh."

"He said something to you?"

"Yes." She glanced at me, then looked away.

"What did he say?" I asked, ready to protect my girl even against my best friend.

Mates before dates no longer applied when it was a man's girl we were talking about.

Jonathan might not know that Grace was my girl, but he would find out soon enough.

"He 'um. He basically gave us his blessing."

The elevator doors opened and we stepped off.

"How?" I asked. "How did he know?"

"I don't know. He's some kind of a mind reader."

"I always knew there was something funny about him."

Grace laughed and my world felt right. More right than it ever had.

I had my girl and there was nothing I wouldn't do for her.

Epilogue
GRACE

One year later

I SAT at my desk in my second-floor guest bedroom turned office and finished up a session with one of my online clients.

Someone else had my office down the hall from Jonathan's and I was okay with it.

This was my office now. My view wasn't the same. Instead of traffic, it looked out over a little pond where ducks tended to flock.

People walked past all hours of the day. Some strolled. Some jogged.

Benjamin and I usually went for a stroll in the evenings.

Until lately, I'd get up early and go for a run in the mornings before the heat made it unbearable.

Right on cue, I heard the garage door open.

It would be Benjamin.

I closed my computer, happy to put the work day behind me.

With Benjamin's influence, I'd learned to compartmentalize work from family.

He usually made it home somewhere between five and seven and that officially ended my work day.

By the time I carefully made my way down the stairs—I always thought of Jonathan when I did stairs—Benjamin was coming in through the back door.

He had a propensity to bring me gifts. Sometimes flowers. Sometimes dinner. Sometimes something he picked up when he visited someplace new.

Today he carried a basket with a handle.

He set the basket on the island, pulled me into a hug, and kissed me on the lips.

"What's in the basket?" I asked.

"It's a special surprise for you."

I grinned. He loved surprises and since he gave good ones I didn't complain.

"When can I see it?"

"You can open it now, but..."

I pulled the basket toward me, but I waited for him to finish his sentence before I opened it.

"But?"

"I should probably tell you why."

"Okay," I said with a little smile. "Tell me why."

"Open it first," he said, changing his mind.

I opened the basket to find two kittens curled up together, nestled on a soft cloth.

"Oh my!" I reached inside the basket and picked up one of them.

It started to screech.

"They just opened their eyes," he said, reaching inside and pulling out the other one. "They're twins."

"I can see that. Silver Persians."

With both kittens screeching now, I took the one from Benjamin and holding them close against me, took both of them with me to the sofa.

Putting them in my lap, I got them to quiet down.

"Are you going to tell me why?" I asked.

"I thought it was time we started practicing."

"Practicing for what?"

"Practicing for being parents."

"With kittens?"

"Seems like a good place to start, don't you think?"

"I think so."

"I'm thinking maybe I'll get us a puppy too. They can grow up together."

"I'm thinking you're a bit ambitious. But five months should be long enough for us to get into practice."

"I think so," he said.

Picking up one of the kittens and looking into its little face, I waited for him to catch up.

"Why five months?" he asked.

"Don't worry. I think it's plenty of time for us to get the hang of being parents."

"Grace," he said. "Why five months?"

"Because," I said. "I have a surprise for you. You could even call it a Christmas gift."

"Now you're just torturing me on purpose."

"Maybe," I said with a grin. "You'll have to get used to that, too."

He narrowed his eyes at me.

"Give me these," he said, taking the kittens and putting them back in the basket.

"Okay," I said with a pretend sigh. "I guess I should go ahead and tell you since you're going to find out anyway."

"Waiting."

"You're going to be a daddy. Probably about Christmastime."

He looked blankly at me a moment, then pulled me up and swept me off my feet.

"We're going to be parents?"

"Seems we're on the same wavelength."

"We'll always be on the same wavelength, my love."

"Yes," I said. "Yes. We will."

Just like some of the best things in life, what had started out as an accident had turned into forever.

Keep Reading for a Preview of Red Lipstick Kisses and Small Town Wishes...

AUTHOR OF PERFECTLY MISMATCHED

KATHRYN KALEIGH

Red Lipstick Kisses and Small Town Wishes

THE DEVEREAUXS
BELIEVE IN FATE SERIES

Red Lipstick Kisses and Small Town Wishes

PREVIEW

Chapter 1
Ava Whitmore

"I just need them to sell their property," I said.

My cat, Medley, twitched his ears and blinked at me.

"I know. You agree completely," I said, tapping my pen against my desk.

Swiveling around in my chair to watch the traffic below on the Interstate 610 Loop, I slipped my sneakers back on. Traffic was backed up, barely moving. The evening sunlight reflecting off the hundreds of windshields.

Moving my office to my twenty-sixth-floor condo had been one of the best decisions I had ever made. When I had leased it, I'd known the second bedroom would be useful one day. I just hadn't known for what at the time.

Sitting in traffic for hours a day was a huge waste of time that I didn't miss even a little.

Turning my phone over, I checked the time.

Four thirty. That explained the traffic. Lost in my work, I hadn't even realized the afternoon had passed. The last time I'd paid attention to the time had been at eight o'clock in the morning when I sat down at my desk to work.

I hadn't been working here in my home office long. Two weeks since I'd left the safety of the corporate office to stay home and work. I still had to go in to the office once a week, but that was so much better. So many fewer hours commuting.

I still had boxes of books and papers I'd brought with me stacked along the walls.

My home office had floor to ceiling windows with motorized blinds that I never lowered. I watched the sunrise while I had my first cup of coffee and then at night, I looked out over the city of Houston with the skyline miles away, but still distinctive.

I especially liked the view from my bedroom where I fell asleep watching cars' headlights flowing steadily. Since I was a little myopic, the lights glowed softly and sometimes I imagined the cars —actually on overpasses—traveling up and down mountainsides in and around Whiskey Springs where I had spent the summers of my youth.

At the sound of a message popping onto my computer screen, I swiveled back around and clicked ACCEPT.

My boss. Clara Miller was a boss that no one liked. Everyone at the office was certain that she had been a mean girl growing up. A mean girl who never grew out of her mean girl phase.

Another reason to be away from the office. Being away did not, however, keep her from pestering me. Anytime she took a whim to check in on me, she expected me to be sitting at my desk.

She had checked in several times a day when I first started working from home. Then, I guess she got bored with it since I was always at my desk where I was supposed to be and only checked once a day. This was the third time today.

My psychology professor would call it spontaneous recovery.

"Hi Ms. Miller," I said. She wanted us to call her Clara, but I insisted on calling her by her last name.

"Ava," she said without preamble. "Where are you on buying the Sterling building?"

Nowhere. "I'm working on it," I said.

"So no progress," Ms. Clara Miller said.

If she hadn't been looking right at me, I would have made a face. Instead, I smiled.

"Some progress," I said, holding up a legal notepad where I had scribbled copious notes. "Several dead ends, unfortunately."

"How hard can it be to find the owner of one house in Houston?"

Harder than you think. "It's hidden under a closely held corporation. I've gotten that far, but it's not easily accessible."

"I let you work from home because you're good at what you do." Ms. Miller glared at me through the computer.

How was I supposed to answer that?

"I'll figure it out," I said.

"If I recall, you told me the same thing this time yesterday."

She wasn't wrong. I had indeed told her the same thing yesterday.

So I didn't answer.

"I'll find out," Ms. Miller said. "And when I do, I want you to bring the sale home."

She logged off without so much as a see 'ya later.

The wicked witch of the west. That's what some of the other office workers called her. I tried to avoid name calling. I liked to hold myself to a higher standard.

It wasn't my fault the nickname came to mind at the moment.

A nickname like that had to be earned, after all.

I closed my computer and to go downstairs for a bottle of water. Medley jumped off his place behind my computer and followed me downstairs. Behind my computer was his favorite place to spend his days sleeping. It was almost like he was silently taunting Ms. Miller. She would never know he was there. It would be our little secret.

I'd been on this quest to find out the identity of the owner of the Sterling building for two days. Clara Miller wasn't going to just come back with it today.

She'd encounter all the same dead ends I had. And, having very few interruptions, I had the advantage, Ms. Miller notwithstanding. Ms. Miller, no doubt had lots of interruptions.

As I pulled a tumbler from the cabinet, Medley sat down and looked up at me.

"Low blood sugar?" I asked.

He meowed once.

As I pulled out a can of cat food and popped the lid, he purred and walked around me.

I set his plate of food down and filled my own tumbler with ice and water from the tap.

While I drank the cold water, Medley lapped up his gravy and salmon.

I glanced at my sports watch. I needed to get in some steps. But first maybe I'd order in.

The kitchen was a place for warming food and feeding Medley.

As far as actual cooking went, I figured that's what restaurants were for. Restaurants were the experts and they had the bandwidth for food prep. I did not.

First I would have to go to the market. Then I'd have to spend hours prepping. And cooking. Or baking. Or whatever the recipe required. Speaking of recipes, I'd have to find one of those first.

I liked the way my kitchen looked. Clean. Nothing on the cabinets other than a vase of fresh white daisies and one of those big jar candles with three wicks that I lit, usually at night.

I sat down at one of the bar stools and opened my phone to flip through my favorite delivery places trying to decide what to order for dinner.

A text message from Clara Miller came in interrupting my task.

She followed me everywhere.

> **CLARA MILLER**
> I found the owner.

> No way. How?

> **CLARA MILLER**
> I have my ways.

I didn't believe her. There were too many dead ends. No way she hadn't run up against them.

> Who?

When the answer came, I was glad I was sitting down.

> CLARA MILLER
> Rebecca Devereaux.

I stared at the phone.

> CLARA MILLER
> Rebecca Devereaux of Maple Creek.
> You probably know her.

Of course I knew Rebecca Devereaux of Maple Creek. The irony of all ironies. I had grown up in the small town of Maple Creek just north of Houston.

Maple Creek was a lot like a smaller—much smaller—small town version of The Woodlands in that it was well... wooded. It was different from The Woodlands though in that everyone knew everyone else.

My high school graduating class had consisted of eighty-six people. Eighty-six. I had been valedictorian. Other than being head of the journalism club, I hadn't taken part in any extracurricular activities. I had not been a cheerleader or in the band. Instead, I had taken college courses starting my junior year.

I had my MBA by the time I turned twenty-years-old.

They said I was precocious. I saw myself as being driven and goal-oriented.

I left Maple Creek, happy to see it in my rear-view mirror.

And I had not been back since the day I'd left for college.

I'd been raised by my aunt and uncle after my mother abandoned me as an infant.

My aunt made sure I was fed and clothed and taken care of, but she left no doubt in my mind that the only reason she allowed me to stay was because of my father.

My father's sister was my mother and my aunt, even though she never came right out and said it, didn't like the idea of another mouth to feed who wasn't her own flesh and blood.

She had three boys of her own and she doted on them. I was an inconvenience.

Somewhere along my teenage years, I'd made a vow to myself that I would never be someone else's burden.

But that wasn't the only significant thing about going back to Maple Creek after all these years.

There was most definitely more.

Red Lipstick Kisses and Small Town Wishes
PREVIEW

Chapter 2
Austin Devereaux

I turned off the autopilot and prepared to land the sleek Phenom airplane.

My copilot, a Labrador retriever with a sleek black coat, was on alert, watching out the front of the airplane.

He was a good copilot. Didn't require me to make small talk and didn't complain.

It was going to be a visual landing with no control tower to direct me in and no staff on the ground.

A perfect day for a flight. Cumulous clouds here and there dotting an otherwise clear blue sky.

I saw the postage stamp of a runway and steeled myself.

It wasn't the small deserted runway that bothered me.

I'd landed on smaller runways many times over.

As a pilot for Skye Travels, I went wherever I was needed and today I was needed to deliver a guide dog.

Although I was a pilot for Skye Travels, I worked specifically for Ainsley Worthington. Daughter of the founder of Skye Travels, she had started her own company beneath the umbrella of Skye Travels.

She delivered animals, mostly guide dogs to people who needed them.

I found it to be a rewarding job in and of itself on top of the already rewarding job of just getting to be a pilot.

I'd known I wanted to be a pilot since I was five-years-old when my grandfather had taken me to the Houston airport and we'd spent the better part of a day just watching airplanes take off and land. It had probably only been a couple of hours, but to me as a five-year-old, it had seemed like forever.

I may have only been five, but I still remembered what he had told me.

"Learn to fly airplanes, Grandson, and the world will open up to you in every way. You'll always be able to get work and you can go anywhere you want to go."

Grandpa, although he had always wanted to fly airplanes, had never done it. He'd stayed far too busy building and running his real estate company. He'd been a passenger on his share of airplanes though. Commercial planes. Private planes.

He was one of the most successful men I'd ever known. Much like Noah Worthington, the founder and owner of Skye Travels, the company I worked for.

They didn't make men like them anymore. The Greatest Generation. They were loyal to their country and they did what they needed to do to be successful.

Somehow they seemed to have more hours in their days than ordinary people. Or maybe they were just better at delegating. Grandpa always had time for me. That was something I cherished more than anything from my childhood.

I'd never gotten to ask my grandfather his secret for success. Something I regretted to this day.

But Maple Creek had been home. My mother, Grandpa's daughter, had married a small-town man and never looked back. They had raised me and my four siblings right here in Maple Creek and no one had known just how successful my Grandpa had been.

Hell, I hadn't known it until I was in college after Grandpa had passed.

I'd been just an ordinary boy growing up in a small-town.

Ordinary until that day in seventh grade when I had fallen head over heels in love with Ava Whitmore.

I remembered the day like it was yesterday. She'd kissed me.

It had been what my teachers called "Retro Day." I vaguely remembered her wearing rolled up blue jeans and an oversized sweatshirt. But the image burned into my brain was of her wearing deep red lipstick, the kind that had that distinctive scent found only in the reddest lipstick. It was one of those scents I would never stop associating with her. She'd kissed me on the cheek, leaving behind a lip imprint that I hadn't washed off until the next morning. And then only because it was smeared and I had to go to school.

For a thirteen-year-old boy being kissed by the hottest thirteen-year-old girl in the school changed my life forever.

She had, metaphorically of course, taken me by the shoulders and pointed me in what I now knew was the right direction.

I'd followed her to college, but she'd been so far ahead of me, I had been left in her dust.

She was taking college classes junior year so by the time we started college, she was a junior and I was still a freshman.

By then it didn't matter though.

By then we—meaning she—had already deemed it impossible for us to have a real relationship.

I had no reason to be nervous coming back to Maple Creek. There was one thing for certain. Ava Whitmore would not be here. She had left Maple Creek and had never looked back.

But anytime I came back to visit, which was rare, I felt enveloped in memories of Ava. Every step I took in the little town came with a memory of Ava.

I might have left Maple Creek behind, but I had never stopped being in love with Ava Whitmore.

There were two constants in my life. One was flying. And second was that Ava Whitmore would always be the love of my life.

It didn't even matter that I hadn't seen her in just over five years.

Red Lipstick Kisses and Small Town Wishes

PREVIEW

Chapter 3
Ava

The next morning I sat in Ms. Miller's office. It wasn't my day to go in to the office, but the situation warranted it.

Ms. Miller had been surprised to see me. Going in to the office on unscheduled days wasn't something I had done since I had started working from home.

I sat down in one of the soft leather chairs in front of her immaculately uncluttered desk with a glass top and spoke without preamble.

"I can't go to Maple Creek," I said. "You'll have to send someone else."

Ms. Miller narrowed her eyes at me. I didn't care if she saw this as a weakness. Anytime Ms. Miller caught any hint of anything she might see as a weakness, she would find a way to use it as a weapon.

Didn't matter. Going back to Maple Creek was not for me.

"I thought you would jump at the opportunity to go back to your hometown. Everyone wants to go back to their hometown. And getting to go for work is just a bonus." She smiled at me. "Right?"

"Trying to get Rebecca Devereaux to sell her property puts me in a double bind."

"Well," Ms. Miller said. "We all have our problems."

"I thought you wanted her to sell us this property."

"You know I do."

"I'm not the one to do it. She knows me."

"And she trusts you."

And therein was the heart of the problem.

I loved my job. I really did. But sometimes I didn't like convincing people to sell their property so that my company could turn around and sell it for investment property. Someone's prized property would be sold for a parking garage or a shopping mall.

Often times they were happy and willing to sell. Grateful to get a windfall on land they weren't using.

I was okay with those situations.

In this one, however, I already knew going in that Rebecca would not want to sell. And me going there to try to convince her otherwise was not only a waste of time and energy, but I was pretty sure she wouldn't be happy to see me to begin and end it all.

"If you like working from home, you'll close this deal."

"What does my working from home have to do with it?"

"You know I was against it to begin with. I like everyone where I can see them."

She wasn't lying about that. It was why she liked to "pop in" on my computer screen several times a day.

"I do my work," I said.

"I don't doubt it," Ms. Miller said, leaning back in her oversized office chair. She didn't weigh over a hundred pounds, but the chair was suitable for a two-hundred-pound man "But. If you can't land this deal, then you aren't ready for the autonomy required to work unsupervised."

"I'm not exactly unsupervised," I said under my breath, then added louder. "You know I do my job."

She shrugged. "Suit yourself."

I could tell by her tone that she had made up her mind. She was sending me to Maple Creek whether I wanted to go or not.

"If I have to send someone else, then you'll be working out of a cubicle."

"You can't put me back in a cubicle," I said. I hadn't worked in a cubicle in years. I'd left my own office, with a window, to go to work from home.

"Don't say I didn't warn you," she said.

As thus I was duly warned.

After going straight home to pack, I was on the road to Maple Creek by one o'clock.

Red Lipstick Kisses and Small Town Wishes
PREVIEW

Chapter 4
Austin

After I finished up my post flight checklist and got my copilot, aka guide dog, aka Scottie, out of the plane, I still didn't have a ride from the airport.

So I called my best friend from high school to come and pick me up.

Reggie had always been content to live in Maple Creek. I had, in fact, never known him to have any aspirations to leave. It actually seemed like he never even considered leaving as an option.

There were a lot of people like that. A lot of people were born and raised in Maple Creek and were content to live out their lives here.

I could not fathom the thought.

Scottie went on alert when Reggie turned into the little airport, rumbling along in his old blue pickup truck.

As the truck neared, Scottie let out a low growl.

"I know," I said, putting a hand on his head. "You've never seen anything like this old truck, but I promise you it's safe. Or at least as safe as it can be. You don't even have to ride in the bed."

Reggie parked next to my airplane, reached across the cab, and opened the door.

"Dog rides in the bed," he said.

"And I know you know better," I said as I held the door for Scottie. "This dog has more education than you."

"Figured," Reggie said with a shrug.

I tossed my luggage in the back, then climbed into the passenger side. The heavy door creaked as I closed it.

"Where are we dropping him?" Reggie asked.

"Good question." I unlocked my phone and checked my messages.

"Why do you even have a phone?" Reggie asked.

"I wouldn't," I said with all seriousness. "But I have to have it for work."

"I think you were switched at birth. Maybe with some kind of cave child."

"Jealous," I said.

"Of what?" Reggie asked, genuinely confused.

I just laughed. Reggie and I had always been tight, but it didn't mean we understood each other. In fact, I could say with certainty that we did not come close to understanding each other.

"This is Scottie," I said after reading my latest message from my client. "An acclaimed guide dog and apparently we are hosting him until his new owner gets back in town."

"Your mother will be so happy about that."

"She won't mind." I put a hand on Scottie's head. "Scottie is housebroken. Doesn't say much. And is overall good company."

"Don't doubt that either." Reggie pulled out of the parking lot onto the highway that led into Maple Creek.

"How long you staying?"

"I guess until I can deliver Scottie."

"Uh huh." Reggie shifted gears and pulled over on the shoulder to let a newer car pass.

"Ever think about getting a new truck?" I asked.

"Why would I do that?"

"Just a thought. Figured a truck from this century might help you get a date now and then."

"If you must know, girls like my truck. In fact, I had a date last week."

"You've got to be lying. I know that no self-respecting girl would go out with you in this truck."

"Who says I took the truck?" he asked. "Besides she runs just fine." He pulled back onto the road. "As long I give her the attention she requires."

"Sounds like you're dating your truck."

"Don't be obtuse."

I laughed again. In some ways it was good to be home. I missed my family and friends.

I liked coming home, but I was always ready to be on my way, back into the large, more exciting world.

Reggie turned off the highway and followed a blacktop road

about half a mile before turning into my family's circle drive. The blacktop road was lined with rows of maple trees that would explode into a magnificent burst of red during autumn.

I always felt a little tug of homesickness or maybe nostalgia when I got here. This had been home for the first eighteen years of my life. It would always be home in more ways than I could count.

"Need help?" Reggie asked before I opened the door.

"I've got it."

"Call me later," Reggie said. "We'll go sit on the water tower and have a beer."

"You make it hard to resist," I said, grabbing Scottie's leash and urging her out of the truck.

Reggie gave me a mock salute, waited for me to pull my luggage out of the back of the truck, then rumbled back down the driveway leaving me in a world of relative silence.

I stood a moment and looked at the house.

Someone had added a new coat of white paint to the outside walls and planted some petunias in the hanging pots on the front porch.

It looked good.

My mother and father still lived here with their three youngest. They were some of those people who would never leave Maple Creek.

"Come on Scottie," I said. "Let's go meet the family. Don't get too attached though. You won't be here long."

I don't think Scottie cared. He happily followed me up the sidewalk to the house.

The house had a wraparound porch, literally going all the way around the house. The upstairs had plenty of room, but no balconies.

When my parents had built the house, my mother was terrified that one of her children might go onto the balcony and jump/fall off. So no balconies.

So no balconies even though a veranda would have worked well with the style of the house.

I knocked on the door. I had a key, but it didn't seem right using it.

Didn't need it anyway.

My mother appeared at the door, grinned broadly, and pulled me into a bear hug.

"It's been too long," she said. "Let me look at you." Holding me at arm's length, she studied me.

"It hasn't been that long," I said. "I don't look any different."

"You need to eat more. You're too skinny."

"My pants still fit and my doctor says I'm good."

"Well, honey, your doctor is an idiot."

Yes. It was good to be home.

"Is this the one you told me about?" she asked. "Scottie."

Scottie barked once.

"He's a good dog."

"I'm sure he is," she said. "Your grandmother is here."

"What? You didn't tell me that Grandma was coming."

"And ruin the surprise. No way."

I went straight into the kitchen where I knew Grandma waited, Scottie at my heels.

Grandma's face lit up when she saw the dog. Since Grandpa's passing two years ago, it took a lot to get her to smile.

Scottie seemed to sense that and proceeded to lick Grandma's face, making her giggle like a schoolgirl.

"Can I keep her?" she asked.

"Unfortunately, she's already spoken for."

"A working dog, huh?"

"I'm afraid so."

"If you ever retire," Grandma told Scottie, holding his head and looking into his eyes. "You have a place to live with me. Don't you forget it."

Scottie backed twice.

If I had more time with him, I would figure out the dog's code and we could communicate.

In the meantime, I gave my grandmother a hug.

"I'm glad you're here," I said.

Grandma had a place near downtown Houston where she still lived. She claimed she never ran out of things to do and that's why she never left Houston. Not even after Grandpa passed away.

I was pretty sure she rarely got out anymore, but no one challenged her on that.

"Me too," she said, then leaned forward and whispered for my ears only. "I'm thinking about moving in. Here."

"You'd leave the city?"

She shrugged. "It's not the same anymore."

"I see."

"Your mother doesn't know it yet."

"I'm sure she'd be fine with it."

I actually had no idea what Mother would think, but it seemed like the thing to say.

"When?" I asked.

Grandma waved a hand. "I don't know. Haven't gotten that far yet."

"You'll figure it out."

Grandma smiled her small wistful smile. "I suppose I will."

I hated seeing her so heartbroken over my grandfather, but they had been a true couple. Meant for each other. If my grandma remarried, I would be shocked.

In fact, I would bet my career on her never getting married again.

"Did your mother tell you?" Grandma asked.

"Did Mother tell me what?"

"Ava Whitmore is in town."

Keep Reading Red Lipstick Kisses and Small Town Wishes...

Kathryn Kaleigh writes sweet contemporary romance, time travel romance, and historical romance.

kathrynkaleigh.com

www.ingramcontent.com/pod-product-compliance
Ingram Content Group UK Ltd.
Pitfield, Milton Keynes, MK11 3LW, UK
UKHW022201231224
452890UK00012B/620